Friends with Benefits

KELLY JAMIESON

Friends with Benefits
Copyright © 2016 by Kelly Jamieson

ISBN: 978-1-988600-02-4

Cover by The Killion Group, Inc.
Interior Formatting by Author E.M.S.

"Again, my favorite trope...friends to lovers, but OMG, this one was done so well. I really, really LOVED this book!!!"
~ **Smitten with Reading**

"...a light hearted romantic comedy that is full of humor and sexual tension and love."
~ **Just Erotic Romance Reviews**

"With great characters and sexual tension and passion that burns, Friends with Benefits is a great story that I would definitely recommend."
~ **Whipped Cream Romance Reviews**
Bookmark:Praise for the Novels of Kelly Jamieson

PRAISE FOR THE NOVELS OF KELLY JAMIESON

"Kelly Jamieson delivers a blazing passionate read that tugs at the heartstrings!"
~ **Carly Phillips, *New York Times* Bestselling Author**

"seductive and bewitching from the very start... Softly romantic and wickedly provocative"
~ ***RT Book Reviews* on Rule of Three**

"Kelly Jamieson now has a permanent place on my keeper shelf and I can't wait to see what she writes next."
~ **Joyfully Reviewed**

"Ms. Jamieson once again gives the reader a richly detailed story that is brimming over with sexual tension, intoxicating desires and intriguing carnal needs that is edgy and psychologically intense..."
~ **The Romance Studio**

"...I love Kelly Jamieson's books and the way that she depicts her characters..."
~ **Sizzling Hot Book Reviews**

1

"What did you say?" Mitch stared at his best friend across the table from him on the patio at Amigos Bar and Grill where they sat having a happy hour Friday drink.

"I want to get married."

"That's what I thought you said." He couldn't resist a smirk. "Is that a proposal?"

Kerri rolled her eyes. "Yeah, right. As if I'd want to marry you."

The breeze lifted the layers of Kerri's silky black hair and stirred the basket of colorful flowers hanging beside their table. She tugged an errant strand of hair away from her mouth and tucked it behind her ear.

Mitch grinned, taking no offense at her comment. After all, marriage was so far down on his bucket list, it was...well, it wasn't even on there.

"You want to get married," he repeated patiently, and lifted his Corona to his lips. What the hell was this about?

"Yes," she said. "And I want you to help me find a husband."

Mitch choked on his beer. "Huh?"

Kerri leaned forward with an earnest expression on her face. "I want you to help me find a husband."

"You've got to be kidding." Was she insane?

She shook her head. "I'm serious. I'm almost thirty. I need to do this now."

She tipped that stubborn little chin and gazed at him with wide blue eyes.

Ah, Christ. It was the puppy dog eyes. He dragged his gaze away from her and focused on the beer bottle clasped in his hands. Then he snorted and took another swig of beer. "Big deal. Thirty isn't old."

She smiled. "Says you, old man."

Yeah, he was a year older than she was. Neither of them was old, not by a long shot.

"I want kids," she said. "You know I've always wanted a big family. Turning thirty makes me realize I better get on with it."

Jesus, she *was* serious about this.

"You're my best friend. You should be able to find the right guy for me."

"No way." He shook his head, leaned back in his chair and crossed his arms over his chest. The bright California sun warmed his face as he took himself out of the shade of the umbrella above their table.

"Why not?" Her lips pushed out into a near-pout and he frowned.

"You can't be serious. That's crazy."

"Why? I'm still single and I haven't had a date in months. I've been too busy with my business to date. And it's hard to meet guys, you know."

"Uh, no, I don't know."

She gave him that look she always gave him when he ticked her off—chin tipped down, head tilted, lips pursed—and he couldn't help but smile.

"I'm just asking for a little help." Her mouth relaxed and she held his gaze, wide-eyed, all but batting those long black lashes at him. He sighed.

"Kerri, I can't help you with that."

"Why not?" She continued the stare down and he started to sweat. He tugged at the collar of his white shirt, although he'd already undone the top button and rolled up the sleeves. His tie hung loosely around his neck.

"Well, first of all, you know my feelings about marriage. I don't believe in it, so why the hell would I help you find someone to marry? It would just be asking for trouble."

"That's ridiculous." She waved a hand. "Just because you don't believe in marriage doesn't mean *I* can never get married."

"Do I have to remind you of the statistics? Divorce rate of fifty percent? Do I have to tell you again all the horror stories I hear at work?"

As a divorce attorney, Mitch had seen the cruel and vindictive things men and women did to each other in marriages gone bad and he swore he'd never go there. Never.

And it only seemed right to prevent his best friend from the same fate. Right? Right.

"It doesn't have to be like that. Besides, how do you expect me to have kids without a husband?"

He looked at her heart-shaped face, eyes wide and beseeching, her pretty pink mouth curved appealingly at him. His gut clenched. Jesus, it was hard to say no to her. He'd never been able to do that and it had gotten him into some screwed up situations. Like the time she'd talked him into kidnapping a leprechaun statue from that Irish pub in Goleta on St. Patrick's Day. Or swimming in the Pacific Ocean at midnight. Talk about shrinkage.

He softened, looking at her and thinking about her with kids. He'd seen her with all her nieces and nephews, playing crazy games with them down on the floor, making them laugh. He'd seen how they followed her around whenever they were together. Yeah, she'd be a good mother. Shit.

"I know your parents didn't give you a great example of a happy marriage." She wrinkled her nose. "But look at *my* mom and dad...married forty years and still crazy about each other."

"They're lucky." He tipped his beer up and drained the bottle, then rapped the empty down onto the table. "And the exception."

Kerri blinked. "Come on, Mitch," she coaxed, still smiling.

He was a goner.

"What do you want me to do?" He sighed and lifted a finger to signal the server that he needed another beer. Now.

"Just introduce me to some nice guys." She flashed a smile, as if sensing his impending surrender. "I'll take it from there. That's all."

He scowled at her. "It's no wonder you can't meet guys on your own. Look at you. You're such a dog."

"Back atcha." Her eyes sparkled. She picked up her drink and finished her margarita just as the server returned with another Corona for Mitch. "I'll have another, too, please." She smiled at the server then turned her attention back to Mitch. "You're pretty homely yourself."

Things had gotten a bit serious for a minute there and Mitch couldn't help but grin at her put down, much more normal conversation for them.

"Not to mention you're a pain in the ass," he continued. "Damn it."

She still smiled, now with satisfaction. "So you'll do it?"

"I'll think about it." He sighed. "I have no clue who I'm going to introduce you to."

"There must be some handsome, single lawyers at your firm that I haven't met."

No way. None of those guys. He shook his head. "Like I said, I'll think about it."

"Okay, but don't take too long. I'm in a hurry here."

"Oh, yeah, I can just hear your clock ticking."

She laughed and moved back to allow the waitress to set her frosty drink in front of her. Too full to pick up, she leaned forward to sip from the glass and when she lifted her head, grains of salt stuck to her upper lip. He reached over and brushed his fingertips over her mouth to remove them.

Her lips parted at his touch and their eyes collided in a weird clash.

He drew back his hand like she'd bit him. Whoa.

They'd been friends for ten years. They'd seen each other puking drunk, comforted each other through painful breakups, celebrated promotions and business success together. "Uh, you had salt on your mouth," he said, probably unnecessarily. *Christ.* He swallowed a groan.

"Oh." She touched her mouth but the salt was gone. Then she grinned. "That's the best part of the margarita."

"I guess you need some salty chips, then." Again, he beckoned the server.

He had a feeling there was more to her desire to get married and have children than just a ticking biological clock, but now that she had him hooked, she was done talking about marriage and was on to something else.

"The painters are almost finished in the new studio." Excitement sparkled in her eyes. "The renovations are right on schedule and I'll be ready to go June first in my new place."

"That's great. It's been a lot of work, but it's all coming together."

"Yeah." She sighed with relief. "Thank heaven for Sela."

When Kerri had opened her own yoga studio seven years ago, he'd been sure it wouldn't last long. Kerri was smart but not always the most organized person, and she made too many decisions with her heart instead of her head. Spouting off New Age stuff about chakras being aligned didn't give him confidence that she was going to be able to manage accounts payable and receivable and profit/loss statements. But she'd surprised him with her success, working her ass off teaching classes six days a week, sometimes as many as three or four times a day, so busy she'd hardly had time to breathe. She loved it and somehow her business thrived. But recently, her lease had been cancelled and her business became homeless. Kerri's sister Sela had come to the rescue.

"It was perfect timing," Mitch said, "since she needed to move her spa to a bigger place. It was nice of her to offer to lease space to you."

"Ha! She didn't do it because she's nice. She did it because she knew I would bring in a whole new clientele. It's a natural fit for both our businesses. Mutually beneficial. This was totally a business deal."

Moving her yoga studio in with White Lotus Spa had been a ton of work, and stress levels that would knock anyone else out. But Kerri, with her serene outlook and Zen-like ability to master stress, seemed unfazed by all the demands on her. Mitch often mocked her for her dedication to yoga, but he had to admit it did seem to work for her.

"She *is* a smart businesswoman."

Kerri frowned, stirring her margarita with the straw.

"Anyway," Mitch continued. "I'm not sure how you plan to fit marriage and motherhood in with a growing business that keeps you busy teaching six days a week."

"I know how to balance. I know how important that is. My chakras are aligned."

He gave her a look and her lips twitched as she continued. "The chakras draw in the universal life force energy to keep the spiritual, mental, emotional and physical health of the body in balance. Yin and yang." She knew damn well how much it bugged him when she talked about all that mind-body-spirit shit, which was exactly why she did it.

"Karmic crap," he muttered, holding back his own smile.

She laughed. "Oh, shut up. You know I'm right."

He wasn't sure how much of all that stuff Kerri actually believed, but he had to admit she did manage to lead her very busy life with serene steadiness.

"So tell me about *your* day." She leaned her elbow on the table and propped her chin on her hand. Her eyes fastened on his face with an interest so genuine, it made him feel good. Important. Warm.

His day. He leaned back in his chair, not sure what to say. His day had been frustrating, discouraging...not stuff he really wanted to talk about right now. "It was okay," he finally said. He looked down at the bottle in his hands.

"Anything juicy?" Kerri leaned forward, brows lifted.

"How about a seventy-two-year-old couple splitting up after forty-nine years of marriage?"

Kerri's slender dark brows drew together. "That's not juicy, that's depressing."

"They were planning their fiftieth wedding anniversary party and the husband started having an affair with the party planner."

She laughed. "Okay. That's juicy."

He smiled back at her, knowing she wanted to hear the outrageous, funny stories he often had, but the reality was, sometimes things didn't seem so funny any more. A couple in their seventies fighting over a divorce just annoyed him. There had to be a better way. He'd been trying some different things lately, other ways of helping people resolve their differences, but he didn't think Kerri was interested in hearing that, so he entertained her with the rest of the story about the septuagenarian divorce.

2

Kerri leaned back in the chair behind her desk in her new office and took a couple of deep, calming breaths before looking around at the bare, sparsely furnished office. The energy was *so* not flowing.

Boxes of papers she'd moved from her old studio sat piled in the corner. Clutter was bad luck and caused stress, but she still needed some new filing cabinets, so the boxes remained unpacked. She frowned at them.

At least the new desk she'd bought was in the right place, facing the door and allowing her to see the entire room from where she sat behind it. That was good. She had yet to move everything from her old space. It would feel better when her plants were there. The green growth would provide some active energy.

She planned to move the rest of her things on the weekend before the spa opened, with the help of some friends. She didn't have a big budget like Sela for hiring movers and purchasing a lot of new furniture, but really, she didn't need much. She had her yoga mats and cushions, her sound system, her computer, a few plants and candles and aromatherapy stuff... It would be easy enough to move it all in one weekend.

She bounced up from her chair to go see what Sela was

doing, and found her sister directing movers carrying in new chairs for pedicures. It was controlled chaos in the spa area of the building where Sela's staff were running around unpacking and setting things up while the painters finished touching up the woodwork and the plumbers installed new fixtures. The smell of fresh paint filled the building.

"Hey, Kerri." Sela didn't look up from the papers she held. All her spreadsheets and plans, no doubt. Sela was extremely detail oriented and was a master of planning and organizing. She liked to plan out her plans. Every small facet of this move had been carefully laid out.

"How's it going?" Kerri asked. "Anything I can do?"

Sela shook her head. Her black hair, cut in a short bob with straight blunt bangs, didn't even move, as perfect and precise as the rest of her. Kerri could see the strain on her face. She'd been working long hours to make this happen. For Sela, failure was not an option and anything less than perfection was failure.

"Come on, there must be something. My studio is pretty much ready and I can't really move the rest of the things over until just before we open, because I need them for classes at the old place."

Sela seemed not to hear her and yelled at one of the movers, "No, no over there! Please."

Kerri watched for a moment, then meandered down into the entrance of the building. She frowned at the stark, cold foyer. It needed to be warmer and welcoming. It needed a better energy flow.

She wandered around, studying the reception area and the waiting room behind it. She approved of the waiting room being hidden from view of those entering and leaving the spa. Her yoga clients would also be able to use the changing rooms and showers. They could enter the yoga studio from a door off the waiting area, or they could go directly down a short hallway and enter from the reception area as well. Many clients came dressed in their yoga clothes, but a lot of her clients were businesswomen who came after work and needed space to change. This was already a big improvement over her old space.

But it still looked cold. Slate floors and sleek leather furniture appeared modern and stylish, but, like her office, Kerri wanted to add elements that would make the room warmer and more serene. A small water feature would offer quiet, cool energy and soft lamps would balance that with warmth and light. She'd really love to add the hot vibrant energy of fire. When she and Sela were "researching" by visiting different spas, they'd been to a spa with cozy armchairs pulled up around a huge stone fireplace where clients could wait for their manicures or pedicures to dry, while flipping through glossy magazines and sipping herbal tea.

Herbal teas. Sela needed to offer more of a selection of refreshments. Just plain old coffee and tea weren't enough these days. She needed bottled water, too. And flavored water.

She went back to find Sela. "Hey, can I talk to you about some ideas for the waiting room?"

Sela frowned. "Now is not a good time, Kerri. Besides, I thought it was finished."

"Well, technically it is, but you know I have some ideas to make it a bit more soothing...to balance the energy flow."

"I think it looks nice." Sela flipped a paper over and consulted another list.

Kerri sighed. "It does look nice, but..."

"Maybe later, okay?" Sela shuffled her papers and gave Kerri a big-sister smile. "You just worry about your stuff."

Kerri nodded and got the message: shut up and butt out.

"One other thing." Kerri hesitated. "The website needs revamping now."

Sela frowned. "Why?"

"Well…because it doesn't say anything about yoga. I thought I could work on it, add a page for my yoga studio, maybe jazz it up a bit…"

Sela sighed. "Do you even know how to do that?"

"Well…yeah."

"We should probably get a professional to do it." Sela dismissed her idea. "Someone who knows website design. And that's not a priority right now. I'll get to that eventually."

Well, having the yoga classes up on the website was a priority to *her*. She wanted people who checked out the website to see that. She swallowed her disappointment. But like Mitch had said, Sela was a shrewd and successful businesswoman. She must know what she was doing. Clearly, Sela didn't need any suggestions from her.

Kerri sighed. It was always that way. Sela was ten years older than Kerri, the oldest of the four Harris siblings, and a natural leader. An over-achiever who'd excelled in college, she'd graduated with her business degree then used her entrepreneurial skills to start her own business with only a little financial help from the family. There'd been a few ups and downs in the early days, but now her spa was the most popular day spa in Santa Barbara.

Not only that, she'd met her husband through her business. He was her accountant, a partner in a lucrative practice, and they now had three gorgeous teenage children. Sela managed to combine being a professional woman with a being a devoted wife and mother. She was the epitome of "having it all".

Kerri let out a long breath. She was almost thirty and had no hope of having Sela's life. Yes, her yoga business was doing well, not surprising to her, but apparently surprising to her family. Sela's spa business had seemed very entrepreneurial, but when Kerri had followed a similar path and used her business degree to open her own yoga studio, with *no* family money, she was proud to say, the family had smiled and rolled their eyes.

Okay, so the money wasn't rolling in, but that wasn't Kerri's definition of success. Her goal was to help people achieve inner harmony, improved health, emotional well-being, mental clarity and joy in living. She was doing all that and managing to make a living for herself.

She returned to her office. She'd call Mitch and see what was happening with the mission to find her a husband. Or at least a date. She grimaced as she called him.

"Hey, it's me. How's it going?"

"Good."

"Got anything lined up for me?"

Silence. She pictured him running a hand through his hair. "Um…well, not really."

"Mitch! You said you'd help."

"Well, yeah, but I just haven't thought of anyone."

"Oh jeez. You know tons of people. It can't be that hard."

"I don't see you out there finding your own dates. There's nothing to stop you from trying yourself. Don't put this all on me."

She paused and twirled a piece of hair around her finger. "You're right." She sighed. "It's not your responsibility. I should be out there putting in more effort." She hesitated. It was embarrassing to admit that guys just didn't seem all that interested in her. It had been a long time since she'd dated and she wasn't really sure how to go about it, other than hanging out in bars, and that wasn't really her scene. "I was checking out some on-line dating services the other day and—"

"Jesus Christ, Kerri. You're not going out with some stranger you met on-line."

"Why not? Lots of people do it these days."

"Forget that bullshit. I'll think of someone. Wait. I just did."

"Oooh." She sat up straight. "Who?"

"Never mind. Just wait till I check it out with him. Who knows, he could have a girlfriend or something. I'll get back to you on that."

"Yes, sir, Mr. Attorney. Hey, I heard a new joke today. If a lawyer and an IRS agent were both drowning, and you could save only one of them, would you go to lunch or read the paper?"

There was heavy silence, then he said, "Ha ha. Gotta go, funny girl. Later."

Kerri hung up, still smiling at her joke. She loved pushing his buttons. Although, that one hadn't got much reaction from him. He was probably so used to her little jabs he didn't even feel them anymore.

Now she was even more impatient, knowing he had someone in mind for her.

It was only a few minutes before the karma ring tone of her cell phone chimed, vaguely East-Indian and soothing. She checked the call display. Mitch already!

"Hey," he said when she answered. "I checked with Trevor and we're going to meet for drinks after work on Friday. You can join us and meet him."

"Awesome! Thank you, Mitch. So who is this guy?"

"He's a real estate developer." Mitch sounded about as enthusiastic as if he were calling to make an appointment to have his chest waxed. "Trevor Simmonds. I know him from the gym."

"Is he good-looking? Successful? Nice?"

"You don't want much, do you?"

"Sorry," she said quickly. "Looks don't really matter."

"But the money does?"

"I didn't say that! But he should be successful. That doesn't necessarily mean rich. If you like what you do and you're happy, I consider that successful, and that's important to me."

"Well then, I'd say he's successful. But as for good-looking, I have no clue. I guess he's not too repulsive."

She nodded. "Okay, so when is this happening?"

"Friday night work for you? I thought he and I could meet for drinks and you could join us. Then I'll take off. You can take it from there. If things aren't working out, you can easily leave."

"Perfect. For a lawyer, you can be a sweetheart sometimes. Thanks, Mitch."

"Yeah, yeah," he growled. "Don't thank me yet."

She laughed, and they arranged a time and location to meet.

As she set down her phone, one of Sela's spa technicians appeared in her doorway. "Hi, Amanda. What's up?"

"That oil you gave me." Amanda's eyes darted around furtively. "I need more."

"Why are you whispering?" Were they doing a drug deal or something?

"I've been using it for some of my massage clients and Sela doesn't know I'm using something different."

Kerri was puzzled. "She wouldn't mind if you changed massage oil, would she?"

Amanda rolled her eyes. "She has to control every last detail of this place," she hissed. "I love her and she's great to work for, but you know her…she's your sister."

"Uh…yeah." Sela *did* have a need for control. "Okay, don't worry, I'll get you more and I won't say anything."

"It's incredible stuff. What's in it?"

"Lotus and rose oil, and some other ayurvedic herbs."

"My clients absolutely love it." Amanda sighed. "So do I, for that matter. My hands feel so soft. I started putting it on after I shower."

Kerri laughed. "No wonder you need more!"

"Have you tried it yourself?"

"Of course." Kerri shrugged. "When I started making this stuff, it was just for my own use. I'll whip up another batch and get it to you right away."

"Got any other magic recipes?"

"Mmm, yes, as a matter of fact. I've been trying some things with different oils. Ginger oil to relieve muscle pains. You might like that. Kukui nut oil helps to repair the skin's barrier functions, and grape seed and sweet almond protect and hydrate."

"I could definitely use that ginger oil for one of my clients. He does triathlons. Does it work?"

"I'll give you some to try. You can be my tester." Kerri grinned and Amanda smiled back at her.

"Just give me the stuff; if it's good, I'll let you know."

Kerri went back to her office, her mind abuzz with essential oils, ayurvedic herbs and most importantly, her upcoming blind date.

○◌◌◌◌◌○

Friday evening, Mitch waited for Trevor Simmonds on the large patio of another bar in downtown Santa Barbara, not far from both his office and the building where Trevor worked.

"Hey, Mitch," Trevor said easily, dropping into a chair across from him. "How are ya, man?"

"Good, you?"

"Had a great day, actually. Closed a multi-million-dollar deal."

Mitch nodded, smiling, but unimpressed by the money. "Congratulations."

Trevor took off his suit jacket and hung it over the back of his chair. The waitress approached them and they both ordered a beer.

Trevor grinned. "So where's this chick you think I should meet?"

Chick. Huh. Mitch checked the time on his phone sitting on the table. "She should be here any minute. Probably finding a place to park her bike."

Trevor lifted a brow. "Her bike? Like, a motorcycle?"

Mitch laughed. "No. A bicycle. That's how she gets around." He could see what Trevor was thinking, picturing a muscular figure clad in bicycle shorts. "She's very environmentally conscious."

"Uh…great."

The waitress set their drinks in front of them with a flirtatious grin for each of them and Mitch smiled back at her. She was hot—long blonde hair, endless tanned legs, great rack. Then he spotted Kerri at the entrance to the patio and immediately forgot about the waitress.

Kerri's silky black hair fluttered around her face in the breeze as she searched the patio for him. The way she carried herself, that perfect posture, made her seem taller than her average height, slim and toned in her yoga clothes. Santa Barbara was a casual city, so she didn't look out of place in cropped black yoga pants riding low on her hipbones and a blue top that wrapped snugly around her slim torso and revealed a hint of cleavage.

He lifted a hand to wave at her and she spotted him, a smile breaking across her face. He couldn't help but smile back.

Trevor turned in his chair to check out who was coming. His eyes widened and his mouth dropped open when he saw Kerri making her way through the tables toward them. He turned back to Mitch and gave him a broad wink. Mitch scowled. Yeah, okay, Kerri was gorgeous, but the guy didn't have to be a pigdog about it.

Kerri approached the table, and Mitch and Trevor both stood up. Mitch pulled a chair out for her. "Hi, Kerr. This is Trevor Simmonds. Trevor, Kerri Harris."

Kerri shook Trevor's hand with a warm smile and took the seat between the men, hooking the strap of her soft leather purse over the arm of her chair.

"Nice to meet you, Trevor." Mitch didn't like the way her eyes sparkled at him. "So what are you guys drinking?"

"Surf Coast Pale Ale." Trevor held up his bottle. "Would you like the same?"

"Sure."

Mitch had to keep his mouth from dropping open. Since when did Kerri drink beer? Last he knew, she despised the stuff. Said it made her feel bloated and lethargic. Something about the yeast.

"So, Mitch says you own your own business." Trevor turned his chair slightly and focused his attention on Kerri.

She nodded and started telling him about the spa and yoga studio.

Sometimes Kerri could come off as a little flaky when she talked about yoga and meditation and chakra stuff. Mitch was used to it, but he wondered how Trevor would take it. The guy seemed pretty focused on the material world with his Porsche and multi-million-dollar deal.

Well, Kerri had said she wanted someone successful. Mitch guessed that met the criteria. He tipped his beer to his mouth, watching Kerri smile and flirt. She wasn't getting too much into that transcendental crap and Trevor seemed fascinated by her, hanging on her every word. Jesus. It was enough to make him gag.

He glanced at his watch. Had he hung around long enough? On the one hand, he had no desire to sit and watch Kerri and Trevor's flirt-fest. On the other hand, he was reluctant to leave her alone with the guy. Which was ridiculous. She was a grown woman and had dated lots of guys, had even had a couple of pretty serious relationships in the past. She could handle herself.

The corners of his eyes tightened as Kerri flipped her shoulder-length layers back and laughed at something Trevor had said. Enough. He was out of there. He drained the beer and set the bottle down on the table, stood and pulled his wallet out.

"Leaving already?" Trevor looked up, his smile indicating he was okay with that.

"Bye, Mitch." Kerri gave him an absent wave. Not even an attempt to convince him to stay a little longer.

"Yeah." Mitch dropped some bills on the table to cover his tab. "I've got a date tonight, so I better head out." With a lift of his hand and a tight smile, he left the patio.

He strolled down State Street in the evening sunshine, oblivious to the rush hour traffic and throngs of people ending the business week. Tourists crowded the sidewalks, meandering in and out of the shops and restaurants lining the street. Two blocks down and around the corner he arrived at his office, in an older Spanish-style building just off State Street. He'd left his car parked in the lot reserved for partners of Campbell, Chapman, Markewich.

He could go into the office and do some work for a few hours, since he didn't really have a date. Kerri hadn't even asked about that. Normally, she'd want to know all the details, but Trevor had obviously been distracting her.

He paused outside the office building. He was edgy, wired, his gut tight. He changed his mind about working. He'd find something else to fill his Friday night. He thumbed the button of his keyless remote and unlocked the door of his SUV. He'd call one of his other buddies and see what was going on. Maybe they'd get some food, find a game on TV to watch or something.

3

Kerri couldn't believe how lucky she was. The first guy Mitch had set her up with, and just look at him! Tall, well-built, handsome and obviously successful from how he talked about his work and the deal he'd just closed. And he seemed interested in her, too. She'd seen the look on his face as she approached the table. It wasn't like she hadn't seen that look before; she knew she was reasonably attractive. But she'd been out of the world of dating and flirting for so long, she'd forgotten how much fun it was.

She smiled at Trevor warmly over her second beer— ugh. Beer wasn't her favorite beverage but she wanted to make a good impression.

"So how about if we go somewhere for dinner?" Trevor was saying.

Yes!

"We could head down to the Wharf...?"

"Sounds good," she said. "But I came straight from work...I wouldn't mind going home to change quickly."

"Yeah, me too." His business suit and tie looked good on him, though. "I'll pick you up at your place in about an hour? That okay?"

"Absolutely." She picked up her purse and gave him

the address of her condo on the Mesa. She practically danced out of the bar and over to where she'd locked her bike. This was going really well.

She cycled home, quickly showered and changed into jeans and a pretty top, exchanging her Nikes for heels. She touched up her makeup, although all she usually wore was a bit of eye shadow and lip gloss, and was just tucking her cell phone into her purse when Trevor rang her doorbell.

He stepped inside and looked around. "Nice place."

"Thanks." She picked up her keys. "I bought it last year. It's pretty small, but it's okay for me."

"Real estate is pricy here, but this is a cute little place."

She locked the door behind them and they headed out. "Cool car." Her eyes swept over the gleaming blue Porsche 911 parked in front of her place.

"Thanks," he said. "Eighty-five grand."

"Uh...really." Okay, she knew Porsches were pricy; he didn't have to tell her how much he'd spent. But financial success was a good thing, she reminded herself.

They drove down to Cabrillo Boulevard, followed it along the beach and turned onto the wharf, the wheels of the car bumping over the wooden planks. Trevor pulled up in front of the restaurant and stopped, got out and opened her door for her, then tossed the keys to the valet. He led her into the cool, dim restaurant. "Should we sit inside or would you like to go up to the patio?"

She shrugged. It would be nice to sit overlooking the harbor. "Outside," she decided, and the hostess led them up the stairs and onto the patio. Glass walls sheltered them from cool ocean breezes but gave an unobstructed view of the jumble of masts in the harbor and the azure ocean. The Channel Islands were faintly visible in the distance, a misty smudge on the horizon.

Kerri perused the menu as a waiter filled their water glasses. Trevor immediately ordered another beer but this time she requested a glass of Chardonnay. She could only drink so much beer. Ugh.

"So. Tell me more about your job," Kerri invited him, lifting her glass of wine.

"I work for Brandon Developers. We do a few different things. Residential and commercial real estate development. We also manage our projects."

"Like what?"

"The new AmTec Center." He referred to a large strip mall just outside the city. "We just finished that last year. We manage the building and lease it to tenants for commercial use. I work in the commercial development area. Did I mention that I just closed a deal worth over two million dollars?"

Uh...actually, he had. "What is it?" She wasn't sure if she really got what he did.

"We'll be developing a new building for Wightman Pharmaceuticals. It's a mixed-use development consisting of a hundred-and-twenty-square-foot, two-story executive office building, and a forty-thousand-square-foot research and development building. We won this project over some stiff competition from other developers, so it's pretty huge."

"Ah." She nodded. "I wish I'd known you when I was looking for space for my business. I had a hard time finding something appropriate that I could afford."

He laughed. "You're too small to be one of our clients."

Oh. She sat back in her chair, nonplussed.

They talked more and continued getting to know each other over dinner. Kerri didn't think much of it when Trevor ordered another beer, and was pleased when he insisted on a nice bottle of wine to have with their dinner. But when he poured himself a third and a fourth glass and finished off the bottle, she started to get concerned. During dinner, he ordered a second bottle of wine.

"Um...I've had enough," she said hesitantly. "Don't order it just for me."

He waved a hand and laughed. "Oh, you can have another glass."

Kerri pushed down her misgivings and smiled, even as Trevor's voice grew louder and more slurred. Other diners in the restaurant started casting glances their way, and by the time they'd finished dinner, she wanted to slink down into her seat.

"You can't drive," she told Trevor firmly as he signed the credit card slip with an unsteady signature. "And I think I've actually had too much to be able to drive, myself."

"Hey, no problem," he said loudly. "We'll just go for a walk. There's another bar just down the wharf." He grabbed her roughly around the shoulders and pressed a sloppy, wet kiss to her cheek. *Eeew.*

"Actually, I'd like to go home. I think we should call a taxi."

He stared at her with unfocused eyes. "Come on, Kerri. It's early and we're having such a good time. And I'm celebrating my multi-million-dollar deal today."

She hesitated, but this was a total turnoff. "No thanks." She forced a smile. "I'll call a taxi. You go on, if you like."

He frowned, then to her astonishment, waved a hand and left the restaurant. She gaped after him, then pulled her cell phone out of her purse and called a taxi.

❦

Mitch waited until Saturday afternoon to call Kerri. She had a yoga class at ten o'clock for an hour and then she'd be free, although she'd probably go to the new studio to get things ready for the move.

"Where are you?" he asked when he finally got a hold of her.

"At the new studio. Just finishing up some paperwork."

"How'd the evening go? You two hit it off?"

She sighed. "Well, at first we did. I thought he was really nice. Then he started saying things that were kind of...I don't know. Insulting."

"Really."

"Well, not insulting, just...disparaging. Anyway. We decided to go somewhere else for dinner and things kind of got ugly."

"What do you mean ugly?" He scowled. Was he going to have to hunt this guy down and punch him?

"The guy's a lush. He was pissed as a newt."

Ah. Mitch leaned back into his leather couch and crossed one ankle over his knee. "What is a newt, anyway?"

There was silence on the other end of the line. "Um...I think it's like a lizard or something."

"And newts get drunk?"

"Mitch..." He heard the warning in her voice.

"Sorry, sorry," he said. "So. What did he do?"

"He didn't do anything, other than get totally wasted."

"Oh. So I shouldn't be watching out for my wedding invitation any time soon?"

Kerri snorted. "Ha. How about never."

"That's unfortunate." He tried to sound sincere.

There was another small silence on the other end of the line. "Yeah. So now you need to think of someone else."

"Oh no." He sat up straight. "I did what I said I would. Isn't that enough for you?"

"Well, no," she said slowly. "Come on, Mitch. You said you'd help. I still need to find a husband."

He shook his head, even though she couldn't see him. "You're crazy, honey. Whacked. This isn't going to work. You can't just find a husband like that."

"Well, I have to start somewhere. You said you'd help," she reminded him again, her soft voice pleading.

Oh shit, here we go again. He swallowed a sigh. "I'll see

23

what I can do. It's not that easy. Everyone I know is either married or already in a relationship."

"There must be somebody."

"I'll see."

After he hung up the phone, he stared up at the ceiling of his office. How was he going to get out of this now?

∽⊘⊛⊘∾

"The guy just wants to spend his daughter's birthday with her."

Mitch leaned back in the chair behind his desk, the phone to his ear, and frowned. "Garth, this custody deal was hammered out and finalized months ago. The agreement was every other year. This is not his year to spend the kid's birthday with her. There's no way my client is going to reopen this."

He heard Garth Layton, the other attorney, give a weighty sigh. "Come on, Mitch. You have to try."

"I can't just go to her with nothing. Give me something here, Garth."

There was a pause, then Garth said, "Okay. He's having some health issues. He doesn't want anyone to know, least of all his ex-wife, so that's all I can tell you."

"Not enough." Mitch shook his head. "There's no way she'll go for it. Health problems. Jesus. I've met a lot of bitter, angry women, but she takes the prize. If I tell her that, she'll say no just to spite him. There has to be something in it for her."

"Just try, Mitch. He wants the daughter for her birthday in September, and Christmas."

"Christmas too! Holy shit."

Again, silence on the other end. "You're a smooth talker," Garth said wearily. "You could talk a hooker into joining a convent. Could you just talk to her?"

There was something in Garth's voice that made Mitch pause. "Okay," he finally said. "No guarantees, that's for sure. I'll get back to you."

He hung up the phone and scribbled some notes on a pad of paper on his desk, then tossed down his pen. He was going to have to meet with Mariah Sinclair. No way would a phone call do in this case.

He ran his hands through his hair. He had no idea what he was going to say to her, but he had to take the request to her and get her answer. As if he didn't know what it was going to be.

He was getting so tired of this shit. Why couldn't people just get along?

He went to ask Christie to set up the appointment. His new assistant was working out great. She was young and didn't have much experience, but she was smart and had a lot of initiative. If she saw something that needed to be done, she did it without waiting for him to ask. He liked that.

"Can you call Mariah Sinclair and set up a meeting with her?"

When Christie stood and moved over to a file cabinet his gaze dropped to her legs. Great legs. Skirt just short enough, and it didn't hurt that she had a rack to rival that of a centerfold model, either. Whoa. Completely inappropriate, he told himself, holding in his grin. He wasn't interested in Christie that way at all, but he couldn't help but notice her uh…attributes.

After lunch with some of the other lawyers from the firm, as they all pulled out wallets to settle their bills, the new guy, Jason, mentioned he'd just moved to Santa Barbara from Seattle and didn't know many people.

"Where's a good place to meet people?" Jason asked.

"You're not married?" Mitch inquired.

Jason shook his head. "Nah."

Mitch studied the man, wondering…without knowing

much about this guy, it was risky. "I'll introduce you to some friends of mine. Why don't you join us for lunch tomorrow?"

"Sounds great."

So Mitch called Kerri again and told her someone would be joining them. Her excitement annoyed him.

"Thanks, Mitch!" Gratitude warmed her voice. "You're a sweetheart."

He didn't feel like a sweetheart. He felt like a bear with a hangover, grouchy and irritable.

◯◦◦◦◯

After the last time, when Kerri had been so positive and then things had turned ugly, she wasn't going to get her hopes up too high. She kept telling herself that all the way to the restaurant to meet Mitch and Jason.

Her initial impression was that he was a nice guy — well-dressed, well-groomed, cute smile. At first he'd seemed surprised it was just the three of them having lunch, but conversation was friendly.

When she found out that he used to do yoga, her stomach fluttered with excitement. This had to work out. It was perfect.

But as the server cleared the table, Jason still hadn't even hinted that he was interested in asking her out. Kerri tried to catch Mitch's eye, hoping he would realize she wanted him to do something, give a little push or hint, or something. But he didn't seem to catch her glances and then the server was bringing their bills. Damn.

Kerri bent down and reached for her purse. They'd been talking about movies and Jason mentioned the new James Bond movie just coming out.

"I really want to see that!" she said, straightening. "The previews look so good!"

She caught Mitch rolling his eyes and ignored him.

Still, Jason didn't make the offer. She was going to have to take matters into her own hands. She took a breath. "Would you like to go see it on Friday night?"

He smiled and gave a little shrug. "Sure, why not?" It wasn't the most thrilled reaction she'd ever seen, but at least he hadn't turned her down flat.

They exchanged phone numbers so they could make plans for Friday night. Well, it was a start. Who knew, things could develop even if it hadn't been a sizzling beginning.

When she got back to the studio, she called Mitch to thank him.

"Don't thank me so soon. You haven't gone out yet. And I gotta tell you, I don't know this guy that well. He only started here a month or so ago."

"He seems nice. So it's something. Thanks."

"But what about me?" His fake whine made her smile. "I want to see that movie too."

"Get a date and come with us. Hey, whatever happened with your date last weekend? I was so wrapped up in my own disaster I forgot you had a date that night too. Who was it with?"

"Oh, yeah…that was…I forget her name."

"Mitch!"

"Oh, Sandra, that's it. It was okay."

"Are you going to see her again?"

"Uh…no. I don't think so. Just didn't click."

"That's too bad. You need someone too, you know."

"Oh no. Don't get any ideas about me. You're the one who's looking. And, unlike you, I don't have any trouble getting my own dates, thank you very much."

"Hey!"

"What? You did ask me for help, didn't you? Wasn't that what this was all about? Or did I misunderstand?"

"Shut up." She gave a little laugh. "Hey, why does the

bar association prohibit sex between lawyers and their clients?"

"Huh?"

She repeated the question.

"Oh Christ," he said with a sigh. "Why?"

"To prevent clients from being billed twice for essentially the same service." She laughed at her own joke as Mitch groaned.

❦

Kerri enjoyed the movie as much as she'd anticipated, and Jason seemed to like it too. He should have been dream date material—polite, friendly, considerate. The only awkward moment had been at the beginning of the evening, when Jason had asked where Mitch was. Apparently he'd assumed Mitch was joining them, and Kerri had explained a little clumsily that it would just be the two of them.

After the movie, she proposed going out for coffee somewhere. Jason suggested a popular, crowded coffee shop near the theater. They managed to find a table, squeezed between two good-looking guys sitting on their left—wow!—and another pair of men on their right.

When they'd ordered, Kerri excused herself to go to the restroom. She brushed her hair and touched up her lip gloss, making sure she looked her best, glumly aware there still were no sparks happening between her and Jason. This date was about as exciting as a dental check up. He seemed to like her and he wasn't running away, but she would have been happier if there had been a little attraction there. Maybe she'd have better luck with one of the guys at the table next to them.

When she returned to their table, another man sat there with Jason. She took her seat and smiled inquiringly at Jason.

28

"Hey, Kerri. This is Matt. I met him the other day at Starbucks. He just happened to be here too, so I asked him to join us."

Ooookay. Fine. She supposed if he didn't know anybody in town, running into a familiar face was nice for him. This kind of reduced the chances of any heat growing between them, though. Oh well.

She sipped her chai tea and listened while Matt and Jason had an animated conversation about a book they'd just read about someone who was both man and woman. She hadn't heard of it, much less read it.

"Oprah picked it this year for her book club," Matt enthused.

"It's like Teiresias, in the Greek tragedies," Jason said. "Since he lived as both a male and a female, the gods asked him to settle an argument about whether males or females get more pleasure from lovemaking."

Matt grinned. "What was his answer?"

"He said females did, and Hera struck him blind." They both laughed. Kerri blinked and contemplated the coffee shop. This really wasn't turning out like she'd hoped. She glanced at her watch and finished her tea.

"Um...Jason...it's getting late..."

His brows rose and he, too, looked at his watch. "Uh...you want to go?" He glanced at Matt.

"Well..."

"Let's just stay a little longer."

She sighed. "Okay. Sure."

But when they continued to talk and ignore her, she started to get annoyed. He'd seemed so nice, but this was just rude. Then she slowly realized Matt had shifted his chair closer to Jason and the two men sat so close they were almost touching as they talked. In fact...they *were* touching. Jason reached out and put his fingers on the back of Matt's hand where it lay on the table. The brief gesture spoke volumes as realization suddenly kicked in.

He was gay!

Shit. She was striking out again.

She leaned forward and smiled at Jason to catch his attention. "I really do need to go." She smiled apologetically. "But you don't have to. I'll just catch a cab home."

"Are you sure?" He barely looked at her. He clearly didn't want to leave. Well, at least one of them was having a good night.

"Absolutely," she assured him. "It's fine." *I'm getting used to taking a taxi home from dates.*

4

This time Kerri called Mitch, and she didn't wait until afternoon. She called him from her studio before her Saturday morning class started. She knew she'd woken him up by the sleepy sound of his voice.

"Thanks a bunch, buddy!"

"Who is this?"

"You know who it is," she snapped. "And I'm pissed."

"I take it the date didn't go very well?"

"Well, not for me. But I think Jason may have got lucky last night."

"Huh?" He paused. "Jesus, Kerr, I haven't even had coffee yet. Don't confuse me."

"He's gay, you idiot. We went out for coffee after the movie and he ran into some guy he knew named Matt, and, well, they kind of hit it off...if you know what I mean."

Mitch was silent for a moment. "So it's my fault that he's gay?"

"Yes!" She paused a beat. "Well, okay, no, but you know what I mean. What the hell, Mitch...fixing me up with a guy who's gay? That is very bad karma."

"I told you I don't know him that well. And anyway, why would he go out with you if he's gay?"

"Actually, I think he wanted to go out with *you*," Kerri muttered, twisting a strand of hair.

Mitch made a little choking noise.

"It's just so disappointing. I didn't want to get my hopes up too much this time, but jeez..."

"Okay, so are you finally realizing this isn't going to work?" He sounded more awake now.

She sighed. "I can't give up already. I've been out with two guys—two! Come on, Mitch."

"Oh, no. I'm not doing very well here. If you're going to ask me for help and then get mad at me when I do it, I'm not going to play anymore. That's it."

She bit her lip and said nothing. She still needed his help even though things hadn't been working out that well. "Okay, it's not your fault," she said reluctantly. "I don't blame you. Really. I still want you to help."

He was silent. "I'll try one more," he said heavily. "But three strikes and I'm out. Okay?"

"Mitch?"

"What?"

"You're not doing this on purpose, are you?"

"Huh?"

"You know...setting me up with guys you know won't work out, just so you can be proven right. 'Cause that would be bad karma, Mitch."

Again, heavy silence. "Is that what you think?"

"You do like to always be right."

"I *am* always right. I don't need to play games to be proven right. Especially in this case."

"Okay." She was sorry she'd asked that. She trusted Mitch with her life. He was arrogant as hell sometimes, also stubborn and controlling, but he didn't play games. "Sorry."

"Are you going to Miguel and Hailey's place tonight?"

"Yeah. You?"

"Yeah. Want me to pick you up?"

"Okay."

"We can talk more then. When I'm awake."

⟡

"So, are you still going to help me?" Kerri asked Mitch later that evening, standing in Hailey and Miguel's crowded living room. She leaned against a wall near the dining room, Mitch standing beside her. Kanye West thumped from Miguel's expensive sound system and a burst of laughter erupted from the kitchen where the party had overflowed.

Her stomach had been knotted up ever since their conversation earlier. She knew Mitch didn't want to help, and she was getting worried that this whole plan might damage their friendship. She didn't want that.

He sighed heavily and put his arm around her shoulders, pulled her in for a hug. "Yeah, yeah. I don't need any of that bad karma shit. I just don't know who else to set you up with. Is there anybody here you don't know?"

"Just that girl." Kerri nodded at a pretty little redhead sitting on the couch. "Who is she?"

Mitch smirked. "You're interested in her? Well, no wonder we're not having any luck…"

She cuffed his shoulder.

Mitch laughed, eyed the girl and shrugged. "I'll find out who she is." He grinned, released Kerri, and moved across the room. Kerri watched him approach the girl with his gorgeous smile, and frowned. Hey, he was supposed to be helping *her* find a man, not trolling for girls for himself. She stood alone for a few moments, watching the pretty redhead succumb to the charm of Mitch's tousled golden-brown hair, his square jaw, his amber-colored eyes and sexy smile, until Hailey came up to her and started talking about wedding plans.

Miguel and Hailey's wedding in five weeks was the main focus of their lives. In fact, as one of the bridesmaids, it consumed a lot of Kerri's life too lately, what with bridal showers, dress fittings, visits to the florist and shopping for decorations.

Much as Kerri loved Hailey, her friend's approaching nuptials just made her feel depressed. She wanted that for herself! Well, she amended, she didn't just want a wedding. The wedding was fun, but it was just a party, after all. She was always amazed how people got all wrapped up in the wedding plans and forgot that they were entering into a marriage. She, on the other hand, would be perfectly happy to elope. She just wanted a marriage. Someone to love, to spend the rest of her life with, to have a family with. And…as a married woman, and some day even a mother, people would have to take her seriously.

She listened politely to Hailey's lengthy wedding talk, keeping an eye on Mitch as he flirted shamelessly with the little redhead. Of course, the redhead seemed just as interested in him, and she watched the girl touch Mitch's arm as she talked, leaning in to hear him over the noise of the music and people talking.

"So what's new at the White Lotus, Kerri?"

Kerri eyed Mitch and his new friend.

"Kerri?"

Mitch laughed about something and Kerri frowned.

"I'm flying to the moon tomorrow," Hailey said.

"Who *is* that?" Kerri turned to Hailey.

Hailey rolled her eyes and glanced over. "That's Allison. She works with Miguel. He invited her tonight."

"Oh."

Hailey smiled. "Looks like she and Mitch are hitting it off."

"Yeah. It does." Kerri scowled.

"Maybe he'll bring her to the wedding."

"Ha. They just met. I doubt it."

Hailey looked at her, then said, "Come help me in the kitchen."

Kerri was happy to leave the room and help Hailey put food out on the table in the dining room. A while later Mitch appeared in the kitchen.

"Should I take a taxi home tonight, too?" Kerri asked him, just a little snippy. "I'm getting used to doing that."

He frowned. "Of course not. Why?"

"Just thought you might want to leave with Alice, or whatever her name is."

He grinned. "Ah. Well, no. I brought you here and my mother always taught me that you leave with the one you brought."

Kerri couldn't help but smile. "Okay, thanks. Just let me know when you're ready to go."

He glanced at his watch. "Any time."

Kerri shrugged. "I'm ready, I guess."

On the short drive home, she said, "This wedding is all-consuming for Hailey and Miguel."

"No kidding. That's all Hailey can talk about. Love her, but man, it's just a wedding. When is it, anyway?"

"Five weeks. You probably should know that, since you're in the wedding party. Have you gotten a gift for them yet?"

"No. Jesus, haven't even thought about it."

"You're such a guy. You'll probably be picking out their gift the day before the wedding."

"Or day of." He laughed. "Don't worry, I'll get something."

She grinned. "I'll remind you."

He pulled up in front of her house and put the vehicle into park.

She started to get out of his SUV. "G'night. And don't forget..."

"Yeah, yeah, yeah." He waved a hand.

"Oh, wait." She turned back to him. "I'm going over to my parents' for dinner tomorrow night and my mom told me to invite you. Want to come?"

"Hell, yeah. I love your mom's cooking. What time?"

"Around four."

"I'll pick you up."

"Okay. Bye." He waited until she got in her front door, as he always did, and accelerated away when she gave him a quick wave.

5

Mitch pulled up in front of Kerri's condo and prepared to jump out to go in and get her the next afternoon, but she was already out the door. She locked it behind her and ran down the sidewalk in a flippy flowered skirt and halter top, her toned body lithe and graceful. Damn, she always looked good.

"Hi." She popped into the SUV beside him. Her unique scent, exotic and flowery, filled his vehicle.

"What's that?" Mitch eyed the huge covered bowl she held on her lap as he put the vehicle into gear.

"Pasta salad. My contribution to the dinner."

"Okay," he said doubtfully. "Let me have a look at that bowl so I remember not to eat from it."

"Hey! I make a great pasta salad!"

He grinned. "Didn't you poison someone with your pasta salad once? On that picnic we had in the mountains?"

"That was not my fault. I bought that salad at the deli. I did *not* make it."

He still smiled, eyes on the road as he drove to Kerri's parents' home. He'd met them often over the years, and he liked visiting them. They made up for his own dysfunctional family, who, thankfully, lived far enough away that he didn't have to see them very often. His father, the poor sap, in the process of divorcing his fourth wife, lived in San Diego, and his mother had moved to Florida. She had never remarried, instead dated an endless series of boyfriends. Much better.

"Mitchell!" Kerri's mother, Angela Harris, put her hands on his shoulders and kissed his cheek.

He smiled as he said hello. "You look as gorgeous as ever, Ang."

She grinned. "You charmer, you."

"Hey, hands off my wife." Scott Harris walked into the kitchen. He too smiled at Mitch.

Mitch jumped back and lifted his hands in the air, feigning nervousness at being caught with Scott's wife.

"I'm so glad you could come." Angela took the big bowl from Kerri. "We haven't seen you for so long. You must be busy at work."

"Yeah. It's crazy."

"Tell me what you're working on now," Scott said. "You were starting to do some mediation work last time you were here. How's that going?"

"Pretty good, actually."

Scott handed him a beer without even asking and Mitch accepted it with a smile. The two men moved out the French doors onto the expansive deck that overlooked the swimming pool in the back yard.

⚬⚬⚬

"I like him," Mom said with a sigh. "You should marry him, Kerri."

Kerri laughed out loud. "Mom, you know we're just friends."

"I know." She sighed again. "But he's such a nice boy."

"He's not exactly a boy. He's thirty-one. And anyway, he doesn't believe in marriage."

"Well, I guess that's not surprising, with those parents. But he'll get married one day. Then what will you do? His wife won't want you inviting her husband over for dinner with us."

"He can bring his wife." Kerri shrugged, helping herself to a spiced olive from the bowl on the counter. She frowned a little though, trying to imagine Mitch bringing a girl to her parents' home. That would be kind of weird. Oh yeah, he'd brought whatshername…with the funny name…Dakotah. Mitch had gone out with her for quite a while near the end of college and they'd come to a graduation party Kerri's parents had hosted. Whatever.

"Need any help in here?" she asked her mother, knowing she'd say no, then wandered out onto the deck to sit with her dad and Mitch.

"Sounds like you're not getting a lot of satisfaction from your work lately," Scott commented. Mitch nodded slowly and Kerri frowned again.

She'd been so wrapped up in all her own shit, with the move and this plan to find a husband, she hadn't really talked to Mitch about his work for weeks. And usually she liked hearing about it. She loved how smart and knowledgeable he was about his career.

"You're a smart guy," Scott continued. "Smart enough to figure out what you need to do to change things around."

Mitch tipped his head to one side, as if considering that.

Both men looked up and smiled at Kerri as she strolled out onto the deck. "What are you taking about?"

Mitch flashed a look at her that she didn't understand. "Just some work stuff. Tell your dad about how things are going with the new studio."

"Oh, yeah, sweetie," her dad said. "How's your business?"

"Going great. Things are almost ready. We're opening on schedule June first. The big grand opening party will be in two weeks. You and Mom are invited, of course."

"Yeah, Sela already told us that."

"How come she's not here today?"

Her dad shrugged. "Some family thing with Doug's parents. She was stressed because none of the kids wanted to go. They all had plans with friends."

It was a challenge for Sela, the control freak, to have teenage children who were now making their own plans and wanting a life of their own, and Kerri couldn't help but smile.

"It will be good for you to have Sela right there," her dad commented. "She can give you business advice, help out if you need it."

Kerri's smile disappeared and her shoulders tightened. "Dad, I've been running my own business for seven years now."

"And doing great," he replied hastily. "I was just saying, Sela's got more business experience, so she'll be a handy resource for you."

Kerri gritted her teeth and almost growled with frustration. She and Sela had the same education, so why did they always think Sela knew more than her? They never took any of her accomplishments seriously, but Sela could do no wrong.

"Can I have some help in here?" Mom stood in the door. "Dinner's ready, we just need to bring everything out."

After dinner, when they were getting ready to leave, Mom handed her the last of the pasta salad she'd brought.

"You keep it, Mom," Kerri protested. "I'll never eat this."

"No, you take it," her mother insisted. "You're single, you need it. And take this bread. And, oh yes, I got some things for you the other day." She left the room and returned with a big shopping bag from Long Drugs.

Kerri peered in and frowned on seeing bottles of shampoo and conditioner. "Mom?"

"It was on sale, and it's the kind that's good for your hair. Moisturizing."

"Mom! I can buy my own shampoo!" Kerri laughed, but inside, annoyance bristled.

"I know, I know, but I saw it and I thought of you. And there are some socks in there, too.

Arms laden with offerings from her mother, Kerri and Mitch headed out to his SUV. They'd just never stop treating her like the baby of the family. She'd bet Sela and her brothers, Justin and Jared, didn't get all this stuff when they came over. Did her parents think she was too poor to be able to afford shampoo and socks? Or that she was too spacey to go out and buy necessities? Geez!

When Mitch drove her home, she struggled to tell him how she'd felt earlier. "I'm really sorry," she began hesitantly. "When you were talking to my dad, I realized I haven't paid much attention to your work lately. Is everything okay?"

"Things are great," he said, eyes on the road. "That's okay. You've been distracted lately."

"I've been a selfish ass, lately. And I'm sorry. We're friends. If you want to talk about any work stuff, just say. I'm a pretty good listener, most of the time.

"Yeah. You are."

Guilt about all the things she'd been asking him to do lately without giving anything in return weighed on her shoulders.

"Next week's the law firm's golf tournament," Mitch said. "Wanna come and golf with me?"

"Sure." Maybe there'd be eligible guys there…

6

On Saturday, Mitch, Hailey and Miguel came to help Kerri move everything from the old yoga studio to the new space. They loaded up Mitch's SUV and Miguel's little BMW and drove over the new studio. As usual, Sela was there working on last minute details before opening Monday morning.

"Sela, you should go home to your family." Kerri shook her head at her sister. "They must not ever see you any more."

Sela smiled distractedly. "Yeah, it's been busy, but we're on a deadline here and everything has to be perfect."

Kerri rolled her eyes. "The world won't end if every little detail isn't finished by Monday morning. Just make sure you're ready for the basics, like nail polishes for pedicures."

"It's not that simple. But I'm just about finished for today anyway. And I have to take the girls shopping for dresses for the party next weekend."

Hailey and Miguel helped carry things in, then left Kerri and Mitch to finish arranging things.

"Thanks for your help!" Kerri hugged her friends. When they were gone, she stood in the middle of the studio, surveying the mess. Actually, it wasn't that bad.

"Just tell me where to put things," Mitch said.

She smiled at him gratefully. "Thanks for your help, too. Let's move the plants over there...no, wait. That big palm tree — can you take it into the reception area?"

Mitch lugged the potted palm out front and Kerri directed him where to put it. She studied the result. Yes, that was a little better anyway. A few more small changes and things would be great. She had another idea.

They hauled her bronze Buddha statue into the waiting area along with another plant and some scented candles. She had tons of candles. She loved the scent and how the warm, flickering light soothed and balanced.

Soon they had arranged everything to Kerri's satisfaction and looked around.

"I guess I'm ready." A thrill of excitement shot through her at the thought of her first class Monday in the new space. It was going to be awesome. "Want some herbal tea?"

Mitch rolled his eyes but said, "Sure."

She went to her office and a few moments later returned with two small cups of steaming, fragrant tea.

The excitement of moving to her new space helped the minor depression she'd been feeling lately. It had been weeks since she'd asked Mitch to help her find a husband, and she had gotten nowhere. Damn, it was frustrating. Patience was *not* one of her strengths.

She sank down onto the hardwood floor, leaned against the white brick wall, and sipped her tea.

They were silent, and she was trying hard not to blame Mitch for all the dating disasters she'd had over the last few weeks. It really did seem like he was doing it on purpose. How could he have accidentally come across so many losers?

"It looks nice in here," he said, strolling around the space

"Yeah."

Again, silence.

"Thanks again for helping me." She stared glumly into her cup.

Mitch slid down the wall and sat beside her, long legs in faded jeans stretched out in front of him. "You're pissed at me, aren't you?"

She turned her head and looked at him. "No."

He laughed. "Yes, you are. I can tell. Just get it out...tell me. The date didn't go well last night, did it?"

"No."

"What went wrong this time?"

"Well. First of all he stuffed his pockets full of sugar packets in the restaurant. Then when we were eating nachos, he grabbed my hand and started licking it."

Mitch choked on a laugh. "Uh...wow."

"Then he called you a slacker."

Mitch sat bolt upright. "What? A slacker?"

"I know! I couldn't believe it either."

"Asshole," he muttered.

"Yeah. I can't believe you've set me up with all these guys and every single one of them has been all wrong for me. Not just wrong for me...like, not even close."

"Wait, hold the fuck up. I didn't set you up with Eric. You met him at the golf tournament."

"Well. You invited me to the golf tournament."

Mitch sighed.

"It's not just a coincidence, is it? You *are* doing this on purpose because you don't want me to get married."

"I don't want you to get hurt."

"So you admit it!"

"No! No, I don't. You're twisting things."

She snorted. "How do you tell when a lawyer is lying? His lips are moving."

At that moment, Sela poked her head in to say she was leaving.

"I thought you left hours ago!" Kerri sat forward. "What about your shopping?"

Sela glanced at her watch. "We still have time. Doug is bringing the girls to Paseo Nuevo and I'm meeting them there."

"Go, go." Kerri waved her hands. After they heard the door close behind Sela, she sighed. "That woman really has to learn to balance. Her family is paying the price for this move."

Mitch nodded. "She is kind of driven, isn't she?"

Kerri studied him. "Like you aren't."

He shrugged. "I balance fine."

She glanced at him, remembering they'd been interrupted while starting to have a big fight.

"Look, Kerri, I know you're not happy, but you can't blame me for all this. You have a role in it too."

She gaped at him. "What are you saying? Are you saying I'm such a loser I can't manage to attract a guy?" Actually that *was* kind of what she was afraid of. Maybe she *was* the flaky loser her family (and apparently Mitch) thought she was, and no guy would ever be seriously interested in her.

"Jesus, no! That's not what I'm saying." He ran a hand through his hair.

"So you're saying I'm deliberately sabotaging things for some strange subconscious reason of my own?"

He stared at her. "What drugs are you on? You're acting nuts today."

"Yeah, I'm crazy, that must be why I can't find a husband."

"Aaarrrgh!" He slid down the wall until he lay on the floor and covered his face with his hands. With his arms up like that, Kerri could see the paler skin on the underside, which emphasized the bulge of his biceps below the sleeves of his T-shirt. He stayed like that for a moment, dragging big, slow breaths into his lungs.

Kerri rolled in her lips and scooted a few inches away. Mitch had a temper, but he'd learned to control it over the years. And okay, she was acting like a bitch and hated herself for it, but the words just kept coming out of her mouth. She was just so frustrated and disappointed and Mitch was there to poke at, take out her frustrations on. A shiver trickled down her spine. Maybe she'd pushed too far. She hated the thought that her best friend was mad at her.

She bit her lip as she looked at him. With his arms raised, his snug T-shirt had ridden up and she could see tanned, ripped abs and a hint of golden brown hair just above the low-riding waistband of his jeans. His hair was all tousled from running his hands through it. She swallowed. Her skin tingled everywhere.

She put a hand on his arm tentatively, wanting to apologize. She knew she could get away with a lot with Mitch and he just laughed at her, indulgently let her act all spiritual screwball, then called her on it and brought her back down to earth. But maybe this time his patience had run out.

His arms jerked away from his face at her gentle touch and she jumped back. He grabbed her hand, held it tightly. His eyes flashed dark gold, his jaw clenched so tight she was sure it must hurt.

"M-mitch...I'm..."

"Kerri." He growled, low and rough.

"I-I'm sorry. You can let go of my hand now." His fingers actually tightened on hers, crushing them, and she yanked on her hand. "Ow! Mitch, you're hurting me! Let go."

His hot gaze held hers as she tried to pull free.

"Jesus, Kerri." His voice still sounded low and rough. "You can only push me so far."

Her eyes wide, she watched a vein throb in his temple. She again tugged her hand away from his but he wouldn't let go, rather pulled her toward him. She set her other palm flat on his chest, hot and hard under the soft T-shirt, to push him away. The warm scents of laundry detergent and male skin mingled as she breathed in, and she trembled.

She pushed ineffectually at him as he dragged her toward him, right up against him, practically on top of him.

"Mitch." She struggled against him, but he was stronger than she was, and his powerful arms held her there. God, he was warm.

One big hand slid into her hair and cupped the back of her head. They stared at each other, Kerri's heart banging against her ribs, tension crackling between them like static electricity, and then he pulled her to him and her mouth met his.

"Mmmph." She tried to protest, shocked to her toes at Mitch's actions. She dragged her mouth away from his. "Mitch! What are you doing? Are you—"

He kissed her again, his hands holding her head against his mouth and her body against his. Again, her palms pushed on his chest, but something happened inside her and to her shock and horror she was...aroused.

The liquid warmth between her legs and the flip of excitement low in her belly stunned her. No! This was Mitch, her friend! She couldn't be feeling like this. And what the hell was he doing?

He was kissing her. And kissing her again. And God, he was a really good kisser, his mouth firm and warm on hers, opening over hers, and her mouth parted for him. Astonishingly, she was kissing him back.

The room spun around her as he rolled her so she lay on her back, and he shifted beside her, almost lying on top of her, his body big and heavy and hot against hers.

His mouth continued to devour her—long, consuming kisses, his tongue licking into her mouth, filling her mouth, and it was so exciting she thought she might burst into flames. God, it had obviously been a long time since she'd been with a guy if she was responding like this to *Mitch*. But she had *never* been so turned on as she was right then, and helplessly she arched into him, her hands clutching his shoulders through the soft cotton of his shirt. And she kissed him back. Her tongue stroked his and he tasted faintly of the tea he'd had earlier and delicious warm male, so she opened wider, letting his tongue in, sucking his tongue, devouring him.

No, no, no. This should not be happening. The thought intruded into her foggy brain. But dear God, it felt so, so good.

"No." She managed to pull her mouth away from his warm, wet one. "Mitch. This is wrong…"

"Christ, Kerri." He buried his face into her neck, breathing deeply. "Christ."

Her hands stilled on his shoulders as she felt him regaining some control, then she pushed hard and wriggled out from under his weight. She scrambled away from him on her hands and knees, half afraid he was going to grab her again, but he didn't. He laid there, one arm covering his eyes, his chest rising and falling with labored breaths.

She sat on the floor, trembling. She put her fingers to her mouth and stared at Mitch in shock, unable to formulate any words. What had just happened?

Finally Mitch spoke. "Jesus, Kerri. I'm sorry."

"You damn well better be!"

"I'm sorry," he said again. "You pushed my buttons…you just kept at it and I just…lost it."

"But, Mitch…"

"I know. I'm *sorry*."

Anger flared in her, hot fury that he would do that, that he would jeopardize their friendship like that, that he would actually use her like that—and he was her best friend!

She jumped to her feet and rubbed her hands over her

face. She twisted her hands together. Then she reached over and punched his shoulder, as hard as she could.

"*Ow!*" He was totally unprepared, eyes still covered, and he jerked up. "What the hell was that? Jesus!

"You stupid, horny idiot! What the hell do you think you were *doing*? You're supposed to be my friend!"

He stared at her, rubbing his shoulder. "Do not ever hit me again," he bit out, eyes narrowed, jaw tight.

Her fury faded as she viewed Mitch in a different light and she took a step back when he stood and moved toward her. She tried to back away but wasn't fast enough.

He grabbed her wrists and hauled her up against him, his body still hot and rock-hard. "I'm sorry," she whispered.

He pushed her away from him and turned his back on her, shoving his hands back through his hair. He stood like that for a moment. "I better go."

"Good idea."

He glanced around at her and the intensity and heat flaring in his eyes startled her again and she swallowed. But he strode out, slamming the door behind him.

She sank back down onto the floor, trembling, legs weak. She covered her mouth with her hands and stared into space.

Okay, that was so bizarre. She had no idea why Mitch had done that. They were friends, for the love of Ghandi. Just friends, never more than friends. It could only be that she had made him so angry he'd lost control, and instead of punching her like he maybe would have if she were a guy, he'd kissed her. So it didn't really mean anything.

Yeah, that was it. It was just the way he expressed his anger.

She didn't even want to think about her own reaction. Holy smokes, she'd actually been turned on! She was wet and aching between her legs. What was wrong with *her*, never mind him. That was a totally inappropriate reaction to a friend who was angry.

She'd never been kissed like that before, never felt that way before, and...never been terrified like that before, terrified of the lust that had surged inside her for her best friend. Even more scary was the way she couldn't stop thinking about it—the feel of his mouth on hers, how his body had felt against hers, the taste of him.

That night she dreamt about endless hot, consuming kisses that went on and on. And in her dreams, she was kissing Mitch.

7

Mitch's anger resulted in a burst of adrenaline-fueled energy and he finally got around to doing all kinds of stupid things around his house he'd been procrastinating on—fixing a leaky tap, repairing a hole in the wall, cleaning his garage. He wanted to be angry at Kerri, but instead he was angry at himself.

What had possessed him to attack her like that? He could guess the answer. He'd been so frustrated by her stubbornness, impatience and crazy obsession with finding a husband even before she'd started in on him with all those stupid ways she had of twisting his words.

Kerri was an intelligent woman. Why couldn't she see how insane this whole thing was? Why couldn't she see this was jeopardizing their friendship? And why couldn't she stop pushing his buttons?

He ran a hand through his hair as he took a break and drank a glass of ice-cold water. He'd been working hard in the un-air-conditioned garage moving things, cleaning. He stripped off his shirt and went back to work in his shorts, perspiration running down his chest and back.

Man, he'd have to phone her and put things right.

Could he put things right, after a kiss that hot? Holy shit. The biggest reason he regretted what he'd done was because now he knew what Kerri tasted like, what she felt like in his arms, and he wasn't going to be able to ever get that out of his mind.

He yanked the ties of a big plastic garbage bag together and tossed it into a trashcan. Yeah, he'd phone her. Apologize. Tell her they'd just pretend that never happened. They were going to the wedding together in two weeks.

Did she realize how hot he'd been for her? If she knew, how were they ever supposed to go back to being friends?

He drew the back of his hand across his sweaty forehead.

God, how embarrassing and stupid. Stupid, stupid, stupid.

Well, there *was* one thing he could do to make sure she never knew how he felt. He could try one more time to set her up with someone. There had to be someone.

His gut twisted. He'd managed to play along with the whole insane plan this long, but it was getting harder.

Marriage was such a bad idea. It wasn't as if he didn't want her to be happy. She was his friend and he loved her. Like a friend. And he knew, better than most people, what marriage could lead to.

Yeah, he'd have to phone her. Right after he scrubbed his toilets.

Not that he was procrastinating.

He grabbed the brush from under the bathroom sink and poured some blue cleaning stuff into the toilet bowl. He was about to start scrubbing when his doorbell rang.

He tossed the brush into the toilet and headed to his front door.

Kerri stood there. She nibbled her bottom lip, her brows drawn down, shadows under her eyes. Damn, she was cute.

"Hey." His voice came out scratchy. "What are you doing here?"

"We have to talk."

"Yeah." He moved aside so she could come in. "I was going to call you. As soon as I finished my work."

Her eyes went up and down over his body. Crap. He had no shirt on and was sweating like a construction worker in July.

"Sorry," he muttered. "I was working around the house."

She swallowed. "That's okay. I interrupted you."

"Thank God." He tried to smile. "I hate cleaning toilets."

"I know." One corner of her mouth lifted.

"Sit down." He followed her into the living room and sat beside her on the couch as far away from her as he could.

She smiled at him, a small, tight smile.

"Look," he said, at the same time as she said, "Mitch—"

"You first," he said.

She shook her head.

There had never been this awkwardness between them before. Shit.

"Okay," he said. "I just want to apologize. I shouldn't have done that. I just lost it. I'm sorry. It won't happen again. And we'll just pretend it never happened. Okay?"

She nodded slowly, her face relaxing a bit. "Okay. I don't want to...I...you're my best friend." Her voice turned into a whisper. "I don't want to lose your friendship."

"You won't," he assured her, although he wasn't sure at all.

"I wanted to apologize, too. I was acting like an ass, as usual. I'm just so frustrated. But it's not your fault at all. You've been a great friend, helping me even though you didn't agree. I'm just being stupid. So I'm sorry too."

He nodded. "I thought of someone else I could introduce you too."

To his surprise, her face clouded.

"A guy I went to college with. He's been working overseas and he's just come back between jobs. Very interesting guy."

She nodded, another strained smile on her face. "Sounds good. Thanks, Mitch."

"And I need a favor from you," he continued. "Help picking out a wedding present for Miguel and Hailey."

She laughed. "I told you you would wait until the last minute. We'll go next week."

"Okay," he said, exaggerating his relief. "Thanks."

"Want any help with your toilets?"

He laughed then too. "That's okay, you don't have to clean my toilets."

"Hey, what are friends for?"

"Not for that," he said firmly, smiling.

<hr />

Kerri tried to keep her mind off what had happened between her and Mitch. A huge desire to talk about it burned inside her. She couldn't talk to Sela, and she considered phoning Hailey, but couldn't bring herself to do it. The whole thing was just too weird, too personal. Every time she thought about it, heat slid over her body and she wanted to squirm.

She needed to meditate.

She went into her new office to the corner where she had now arranged cushions and scented candles. She turned on the soft music, dimmed the lights, lit a candle and sat down, folding her legs gracefully into the lotus position. She took a deep breath.

People took breathing for granted. Sure, it was a simple thing, but it was life-giving. The primary source of prana. It affected mind, body and spirit. Every inhalation brought oxygen into the body and began the transformation of nutrients into fuel; every exhalation purged the body of toxic waste, carbon dioxide.

She inhaled, allowing her belly to fill with air, drawing air deep into her lower lungs, then exhaled, allowing her belly to deflate. She smoothly repeated the breathing several times. Then she breathed air into her belly and expanded her chest, allowing her rib cage to open outward…and…exhaled.

Breathing affected a person's state of mind — excited or calm, tense or relaxed, confused or clear. She drew in another long, slow exhalation, felt her heart rate slowing.

"Feeling relaxed?" a voice asked from her office door.

She opened her eyes and saw Mitch standing there. Immediately her body tensed again. Damn.

"Not really." She blew out her breath and rose reluctantly to her feet. "What are you doing here?"

He grinned, but with a hint of uncertainty. "I was going to call but I thought I'd swing by and check things out."

"What do you think?" She couldn't help it, she was anxious for Mitch's approval.

"It looks great. How are things going? Everyone showing up for class?"

She nodded, excitement rippling through her. "Yes. It's been wonderful. Everyone loves the new space. Reaction has been very positive so far. They also like all the parking nearby. That was another problem at the old place."

He smiled. "Maybe I should come check out a class."

"Yes, you should! I keep telling you, you need to come to class. Yoga would be good for you. It would help with all your stress."

"What stress?"

She snorted. "Okay, it would increase your flexibility."

"Are you talking physically or mentally?"

"Both." She rolled her eyes. "It would also make you feel more at peace in your life."

"Hey, I'm peaceful."

She sighed. "How many hours did you work last week?"

"Uh...I don't know."

"Yes, you do."

"Okay, it was about fifty, fifty-five."

"Mitch! That's insane!" She shook her head

"Anyway," he said, changing the subject, "I was just going to let you know that I talked to Liam, and we're going to get together on Friday. I said you might come too. He remembers you from college."

She frowned. "I know him?"

He shrugged. "You didn't know him very well. He was in a few classes with me. He's a journalist and he's been working in the Middle East. Liam Moffatt."

"Oh. Cool." She shook her head. "The name doesn't ring a bell."

"That's okay. We're going to go for a drink after work on Friday."

"Same deal?" She grinned and he nodded.

"Yup. We'll meet you at Amigo's around five-thirty."

"Okay. I can do that. I'm meeting Hailey, Laurel and Melissa later that night. We're celebrating Hailey's last days of being single."

"Great. Now, to repay me, you need to come help me pick out a wedding present for Miguel and Hailey."

"Oh." She glanced at her watch. "Right now?"

"If you can. I'm taking a late lunch."

This was the first time they'd seen each other since he'd apologized for kissing her. They'd agreed to pretend it never happened, but it wasn't that easy. For some reason, she kept looking at his mouth. Then uncomfortably looking away. Such a nice mouth...no! She shouldn't go with him.

"Okay, I guess I can do that. I'll just let Sela I'm going out for a while."

She grabbed her purse from behind her desk and they walked out front. She saw the glances of appreciation Mitch received from both customers and staff as they passed by the spa, and scowled. He was such a pain in the ass sometimes, but he was gorgeous and, of course, that's all they saw.

She crossed over to Sela, standing behind the reception counter with Belinda, while she showed her how to use the new computer. "Just going out for a bit with Mitch."

Sela frowned. "You're going out? There are a million things to do to get ready for the big grand opening party Saturday night."

Kerri sighed. "I know, but every time I ask what I can do to help, you won't let me."

"Well, you have some things in your studio to do, don't you?"

You're not my boss, the voice inside Kerri's head said, sounding childish. "I won't be long," she said aloud, quietly, and led the way out of the building, with Mitch following behind.

"What was that?" he asked, amusement shading his voice.

"What? Sela?"

"Yeah. Jeez. She cracking the whip over you now that you two are in the same building?"

She sighed. "Well, she is a bit of a Type A. She has lists and schedules and spreadsheets. I don't have that much to do, not as much as she does, but when I offer to help she just says no. Has to do it all herself."

He grinned. "Where to?"

"They're registered at Dinardo's. Didn't you know that?"

"I have no clue." He started his vehicle. "That's in Montecito, isn't it?"

"Yup."

They drove out Coast Village Road beneath a cloudless

California-summer sky, palm fronds tossing in a gentle off-shore breeze. At the store where their friends had registered, it was easy enough to check the registry and make a decision.

"What did you get them?" Mitch asked.

"I got them the big pottery bowl. I know Hailey really wanted that for the kitchen. It's gorgeous."

"I can't believe the prices of some of those things."

"They're designed by some artist Hailey likes."

He nodded. "So those sushi dishes will be okay?"

"Oh yeah, they'll love them. Don't worry."

He nodded and they got back in the SUV. "Did you have lunch?" he asked, pulling out into traffic.

"Um…" He was going to offer to take her for lunch, and for the first time in her life, she didn't want to have lunch with him. Squirmy and restless, all she wanted was to get back to her studio and retreat into meditation. She was so aware of him, big and muscular in the seat beside her in the vehicle, taking up all the space and, it felt like, all the oxygen. He'd turned back the cuffs of his dress shirt to expose his strong, lean wrists, lightly covered with dark gold hair, his fingers long and firm on the steering wheel.

She swallowed. "Um, yeah, I did," she lied. "I'd better get back."

She sensed him glancing sideways at her, but he said nothing and drove straight back to the studio, dropping her off out front.

"Thanks for the help. I'm clueless when it comes to shit like that."

She forced a smile. "I know, but you can't help it. You're a guy."

He smiled back, his smile, too, looking a little unnatural. "So I'll see you Friday after work."

"Oh yeah. I almost forgot about that. Great. See you then."

She jumped out of the SUV and waved as she ran

lightly up the front steps, not waiting to watch him drive away. Once inside, she sagged against the door, but straightened immediately when a customer walked out of the waiting area.

She scurried into her office, dropped her purse on the floor and sank into her chair, burying her face in her hands.

Nothing was supposed to change. The big stupid idiot. This was all his fault. Why the hell did he have to kiss her like that and mess everything up? Now, everything had changed.

She worked herself into a good frenzy of anger against Mitch, then finally sat down in her calm oasis in the corner of the room and resumed her yogic breathing.

An hour later, she went to find Sela. Sela hadn't said anything about the statue and plants and candles Kerri had put in the reception and waiting areas. Maybe she liked them.

"So have you thought any more about my ideas for the waiting room?" Kerri asked her sister.

"No. I actually forgot. But I thought I told you, it looks fine. We don't need to spend any more money, that's for sure." She grimaced.

Sela had had a lot of expenses because of this move, and now she was going all out for their grand opening party.

"It wouldn't cost a lot. We just need a little water fountain, and I could pick up some different herbal teas that we could serve. I think a couple of lamps would help too. It would soften the light. Improve the energy flow. It will be good for business." She had to appeal to the bottom line to get to Sela.

"Energy flow!" Sela snorted. "Come on, Kerri. Nobody cares about energy flow."

Kerri sighed. "You *should* care." She flipped her hair back. "If your customers feel the harmony, the life energy, they'll want to come back. They'll tell other people. It will happen, believe me."

Sela just laughed. "Go on," she said, not unkindly. "Go do your classes or whatever. I have to call the caterer with some last details about the food for the party."

Kerri paused, wanting to say more, but Sela had already turned away, on some other pressing mission. Damn. She had good ideas, she knew it, and she believed in the flow of energy, harmonizing mind, body, spirit. She'd just have to concentrate on her own little world and do her best with that.

8

Friday afternoon was not when Mitch would have chosen to meet with Mariah Sinclair. Christie had done what she could to find another time, but Ms. Sinclair was not exactly accommodating. Not to mention, she was extremely displeased about having to come in and see her lawyer yet again about a custody agreement she thought had been settled months ago, after long and acrimonious battles in court.

"Bob is requesting that we alter the agreement. I believe it's a one-time thing," Mitch explained. "He knows this year is not his year to have Cassandra for her birthday or Christmas, but he's making a special request to alter the agreement."

She stared at him coldly. "No."

He sighed inwardly. "I know there's no reason that you have to do this." He leaned forward. "But I believe he does have reasons for making the request. I'm not privy to the details, but I've been asked to take the request to you for consideration. I just ask that you do consider it."

"No." Her eyes were hard. "That asshole has no right to ask this now. After what he did. And what we went through." She closed her eyes briefly. "I can't believe he's doing this, actually. He's probably just trying to torment me. Well, it won't work. I'm saying no, and that's it."

Mitch looked at her. "They'll probably take it to court if he wants it badly enough. Do you want to go through that again?"

She returned his look. "Of course not. But you know what to do. Cassandra's birthday is only a month away. You can easily stall things longer than that."

Mitch's gut tightened. He knew what she was asking him to do. He swallowed, his mouth suddenly dry, but he nodded. "I'll let you know the outcome of my discussion with Bob's counsel."

As the door closed behind her, he sank back into his chair and closed his eyes. Damn. He had a really bad feeling about this. And these bad feelings seemed to be happening more and more often. The adrenaline rush he used to get from arguing, from pitting his intelligence and skill against a challenging adversary, and winning, wasn't there very often any more.

He needed a drink. He glanced at his watch. Almost time to meet Kerri and Liam. Not that that was going to be a real fun time, but at least there was alcohol involved.

Kerri ordered a margarita and looked across the table at Liam. He wasn't gorgeous but he had a tough, kind of world-weary air about him. She didn't remember him at all from college, although he said he recalled her.

"So, Mitch said you've been working in the Middle East." She dipped her straw in and out of her drink. Liam smiled faintly. "That must have been a life-altering experience."

"Yeah." The corners of his mouth dipped down. "Most definitely."

He talked about some of the places he'd been and the

things he'd covered — fascinating, if a little depressing. The world was really a mess in some ways.

"So why'd you come back?"

"I need some normalcy in my life. I think I just burned out. So I'm doing some freelance work for now. Staying at my parents'."

Hmm. A thirty-one-year-old guy living at home. Probably just temporary until he figured out what to do next. She hoped.

"You should come to one of my yoga classes. You might find it helps. The goal of yoga is to unify mind, body and spirit, to create a balance in the body, open and purify the energy centers. It might improve your health, emotional well-being, mental clarity...your joy in living."

He just looked at her for a long moment. She smiled. Mitch hated all that spiritual stuff, but what the heck, maybe it would help this guy who had clearly seen a lot of suffering.

"Yeah," he said slowly. "Maybe I should try that."

Mitch rolled his eyes but Kerri ignored him. She smiled again. "Here's my card. You can call me or the studio to find out class times. We just moved into a great new space."

He took the card and smiled back at her.

"Time for me to go." Mitch pushed his chair back abruptly. He'd been awfully quiet during the whole conversation.

"Where are you off to?" Kerri asked, not minding that he was going. She'd felt strangely self-conscious while he was sitting there watching her. And he *had* been watching her. His eyes had barely left her the entire time.

"Meeting up with the guys at Good Sports to watch the game."

"Okay, have fun."

"You two aren't...together, are you?" Liam asked after Mitch had left.

"Oh, no! No, we're just friends. We've been friends for years."

"Ah. Then it would be okay if I asked you out sometime?"

Kerri grinned. "It would be more than okay. I would like that."

"Tomorrow night?"

"Oh, I'm so sorry, but my sister and I are hosting a big grand opening party for the new spa tomorrow night."

"How about Sunday night? We could have dinner. Do you like seafood?"

"I love seafood. That sounds great. You have my number." She nodded at the card on the table, then glanced at her watch. "I guess I should get going. I'm meeting some friends in a little while and I still need to go home and change."

She got out her purse, but Liam held up a hand. "Let me get it. Although, I think Mitch left enough money to cover everything."

Trust Mitch. He was always generous with his money. Good thing he had lots. She didn't know how much he made exactly but she knew it was a lot.

She shrugged and held out her hand to Liam. "Nice seeing you again. We'll talk next week."

ᐧᐧᐧᐧ

"Everyone looks so young!" Kerri looked around at people who barely seemed old enough to legally be in the bar. The bass of the music vibrated through her body. She and her friends hadn't been to Ventana's for a long time.

"Oh come on, we're not that old," Hailey said. They found a table in the back with room for four and settled in.

In no time, guys were hitting on all of them.

"I can't believe this!" Hailey wailed. "I'm getting married in two weeks! *Now* the guys notice me!"

Kerri, too, was surprised. Maybe a bar wasn't the best place to meet guys, but it was definitely effective. She loved dancing, so she took advantage of the male interest a few times to dance with different guys. But yet...it seemed hollow. She wasn't sure why. Maybe she really was too old for this kind of scene.

She returned to the table and her glass of wine, feeling empty and a bit let down.

"Oh man," Hailey said suddenly. "I can't believe this."

"What?"

"Miguel's here. Over there! With the guys! This was supposed to be a girls' night out!"

Kerri searched the room and spotted Miguel with his posse of friends, including, yes, Mitch. The guys hadn't seen them yet. They stood at the bar, attracting considerable female interest, especially Mitch. He was the tallest, so he stood out, but he was also completely unaware of the interest in him. Kerri watched as he accepted the beer from the female bartender with a smile and tipped it up to his lips, turning to survey the room. Unerringly, like a heat-seeking missile, his eyes immediately met hers across the room. Her body tightened.

It was as if he'd reached out and touched her. For a long moment they just looked at each other. Then she lifted a hand.

While Mitch spoke to the others and gestured to the girls, Kerri put her hands to her hot cheeks. "Why did they come here of all places?"

Hailey glanced at her. "Hey, it's okay. I don't mind that much." They all shifted around the table to make room for more chairs so the guys could join them.

Mitch ended up sitting beside Kerri.

"Hey," he said. "How was your date?"

"It wasn't a date," she answered shortly. "What are you guys doing here? I thought you were going to watch the game."

"We did." He shrugged. "Dodgers lost. Nothing was going on there so we came here."

"But why did you come *here*? It's supposed to be Hailey's night out."

He raised his brows and looked at her.

"How is she supposed to have fun with her fiancé here?" Kerri continued heatedly.

"What exactly was she planning to do?" He lifted one brow, giving him that goddamn devilish charming look. Damn him.

Kerri scowled. "Nothing, of course. I'm just saying."

He smiled, then deliberately turned away from her to talk to Hailey.

Kerri fumed sulkily. Although she'd protested on Hailey's behalf, she was the one who didn't want Mitch there tonight. Damn him again.

She finished her wine and searched the bar for a waiter so she could order another drink. While she waited, she gazed around the room and tapped her fingers on the table. Then, one of the guys she'd danced with earlier appeared and asked her to dance again.

She jumped to her feet and ignored Mitch as she took the man's hand and followed him onto the dance floor. Mitch was busy talking to Hailey but she knew he'd noticed her leave.

The guy, whose name she'd forgotten, was okay-looking and pleasant and thankfully a good dancer, and he seemed surprised that this time Kerri was so much more animated. She laughed and flirted her way through that song and another one, tossing her hair back and smiling into his eyes. Oh yeah, his name was Paul. As they moved around the dance floor, she glanced back at her table.

Mitch wasn't there.

She pressed her lips together, then smiled at Paul again. The music changed to a slow song and she let him pull her close for the next dance.

Where was he, damn it?

Letting her eyes move around, she spotted Mitch on the dance floor. With Laurel.

Well. Mitch and Laurel were friends, too. It was totally okay if they danced together. She forced herself not to look at them. What did she care if two of her friends danced together?

After the slow dance, she excused herself from Paul. She really wasn't interested in him, and didn't want to give him the wrong idea. With a smile and thanks, she returned to the table and the full glass of wine that had appeared there while she was dancing.

She gulped back some of the drink, unable to stop her eyes from seeking and finding Mitch and Laurel still dancing. She forced herself to join in the conversation between Hailey, Miguel and his best man, Jason. Moments later, Mitch and Laurel returned and joined in too.

"Are you mad that we came here?" Miguel asked his fiancée.

She laughed. "Of course not." She put her arms around his neck and kissed his mouth. "I love it that you're here."

Mitch shot a glance at Kerri and she shifted in her seat.

9

Mitch leaned over to Kerri. "Something wrong? Didn't things go well with Liam?"

She smiled tightly. "Things went fine, actually. We're going out for dinner."

"Great," he lied. "He's a pretty interesting guy, isn't he?" He turned to the others. "Do you guys remember Liam from college? Liam Moffatt."

"Hey, I remember him," Hailey said. "I was pretty hot for him in our last year." Miguel frowned. "He was in one of my classes. Then he disappeared."

"He's been working in the Middle East," Mitch told them. "Kerri's going out with him."

"Get out of here!" Hailey exclaimed. "That was fast."

Kerri nodded and smiled.

"Thanks to me," Mitch added.

Kerri scowled.

Man, she was in a bitchy mood tonight. What was her problem? Or, maybe he didn't want to think too much about that. Hey, he'd said they'd pretend like it never happened. He was holding up his end, but she apparently had issues with it.

"Yup, Kerri can't get her own dates, so I've been helping her out."

As soon as the words left his mouth, regret sliced through him. When he saw the hurt expression on her face, he really regretted it. But it was too late.

"Shut up," she hissed.

But Laurel heard and picked up on it. "You're fixing her up with guys? Hey, why not me? I need a man, too."

"Oh, come on." Mitch smiled at Laurel. "You don't need any help."

Laurel smiled back at him. Kerri sat beside him fuming. Damn, everything he said made it worse.

"Do you mind?" she said to him in a low voice.

He looked at her. Yeah, he was sorry, but no way was he saying so.

"Hey, I've got a new one," Kerri said, louder. "What's the difference between a dead dog in the road and a dead lawyer in the road?"

Everyone waited expectantly.

"Skid marks in front of the dog!"

They all laughed, just buzzed enough that the bad joke was hilarious. Mitch smiled wryly.

"Hey, Laurel, it's late and you're the DD," Kerri said. "You almost ready to go?"

"Noooo!" everyone cried. Kerri smiled, but Mitch could see she really wanted to leave. The idea of offering to drive her home entered his head, but she was being such a pain in the ass tonight—nah. Let her wait.

A while later, he came back from the washroom and found a strange guy sitting in his chair talking to Kerri. Again, she was laughing and flirting with him, doing the hair toss thing, like she had been with that asshole on the dance floor earlier. She glanced up at him, standing there, and the guy looked up too and said, "Oh sorry, am I in your seat?"

"That's okay," Kerri said quickly. "Mitch will find another chair."

He narrowed his eyes but said nothing, and moved

around the table to squeeze a chair in between Miguel and Jason.

He watched Kerri talk to the guy. This was what she wanted. She wanted to find a husband and here was a guy. He should be happy. If she met someone now it would take all the pressure off him and things could go back to normal between them.

Hell, no. This guy wasn't even close to good enough for her. His teeth were too big and too white. He must bleach them. Or maybe they were veneers. What a douche.

He looked around the bar, trying to keep his eyes off Kerri, tapping his hand restlessly on the back of Jason's chair.

"Would you stop that, man? You're making me nervous," Jason said.

"Sorry." Mitch removed his hand from the chair. "Listen, I'm outta here."

"Okay, no problem."

He said good night to the others, but ignored Kerri, engrossed in conversation with the stranger. But as he turned away from the table, pulling his keys out of his pocket, she called to him.

"Are you leaving, Mitch?"

He turned. "Uh-huh." He waited. If she wanted a ride, she'd have to ask.

And he waited. Then she said, "Okay. See you tomorrow."

He turned and walked out, unaccountably pissed off. All the way home he kept thinking about her with that guy. Would she see him again? Would she leave with him? Fuck. Then he was pissed off at himself for even thinking about it.

He didn't sleep very well that night.

Mitch glanced at his watch. Time to shave and change

into his suit, then he'd head over to the spa to see if he could help get ready for the party. Sela was probably cracking the whip and Kerri was no doubt going crazy.

He ran a hand over his smoothly shaven face, tossed on a light splash of aftershave, and dressed in the suit he'd chosen to wear to the party. Okay, ready to go.

When he walked into the spa and laid eyes on Kerri, his jaw dropped. Jesus. She must have bought a new dress for the soiree. He'd never seen her look like that.

Her glossy black hair, usually casual and flippy, had been styled into sexy, messy pieces. And the dress...oh man.

Tiny black straps crisscrossed her bare back, revealed by the low cut dress. And then she turned and damn, it was cut low in front too. Very low. She had cleavage. Really nice cleavage. Funny that. Kerri had an awesome body, lithe with long, toned muscles from her yoga, but he'd never noticed her cleavage before. Well, okay, truth be told, he had...but not like this. She didn't have big breasts, but the dress really showed off their perfect roundness and gleaming golden skin. He had to shove his hands in his pockets against the urge to reach out and touch.

The short skirt fluttered around her knees and showed off her legs, and a pair of black spiky heels looked dangerous. She had on more makeup than usual, her blue eyes shadowed and huge, lips shiny.

She smiled coolly at him, although a touch of nervousness edged her smile. "What are you doing here already?"

"Hello to you too." He wanted to tell her how great she looked but his throat had closed up and he couldn't get the words out. "Uh...I came to help."

"Oh. Thank you." She picked up a big floral arrangement and he tried to say, "I'll take that," but could only hold out his arms. She handed him the flowers. "Can you put those on the small table over there?"

71

He watched her climb up onto a chair to hang a bunch of silver balloons, flashing some smooth leg, and he swallowed.

Oh for God's sake. It was *Kerri*.

"Want me to do that?"

"Sure," she said with relief. "You're taller, you can probably reach."

He did so easily and she directed him where to hang the other bunch.

"So um…how late did you stay last night?" he asked.

"Too late." She grimaced. "Everyone wanted to party."

"Yeah, I could see that." He paused, tried again. "How many people are you expecting tonight?"

"We had replies from about a hundred."

"Wow. Where are you going to put them all?"

"We can overflow into the studio if we need to. But a party is always better when it's crowded."

Kerri's parents arrived a short time later and, as usual, greeted him warmly. Angela Harris looked gorgeous in a stunning midnight blue dress, although not as spectacular as her daughter.

As more guests arrived, Mitch trailed around, following Kerri as she worked the crowd. She moved easily from group to group, chatting and laughing. She charmed clients and potential clients, both hers and Sela's. They returned her dazzling smiles, laughed at what she said to them, responded to her vibrant energy. Yet to him, she was acting all frigid, ignoring him and talking to everyone else.

This was no damn good. They were friends. Yeah, okay, he'd screwed up, but he'd tried to make amends by setting her up with another guy like she'd wanted, and he was trying hard to pretend it never happened. What the hell was wrong with her?

He went to stand beside Kerri as she waited at the bar for a drink. Mitch requested a beer. He took a deep breath and inhaled the scent of her, spicy and exotic. "So," he said. "You get lucky with any of those guys that were all over you last night?"

Kerri looked at him. "Yeah," she said. "I took them *all* home with me. We had an orgy."

Normally he would have laughed at her outrageous comment, but lately his sense of humor had done a disappearing act when it came to Kerri. He made a noise of disgust.

"What?" She eyed him over the glass of wine the bartender had handed her. "You asked a stupid question."

He shook his head. "Actually, I was serious. You're looking for a husband and those guys seemed interested in you."

"You said they were 'all over me'."

"Whatever." He waved a hand.

She sighed. "I wasn't interested in any of those guys."

"You seemed pretty interested last night. There was a lot of hair flipping and eyelash batting going on."

"What!" She gaped at him incredulously. He couldn't help but smile. "There was not!"

"Oh, yes there was. You were the champion hair flipper last night."

She scowled and lifted her wine glass to her mouth, taking a big gulp. Her hand rose and he thought she was actually going to flip her hair back, but then she dropped it to her side as she apparently became aware of what she was doing. His lips twitched. She took in a deep breath and let it out slowly.

"I know you're mad, Kerr," he said softly. "Why don't you just tell me and get it over with. At least then I'll know what I've done."

She peered up at him and her crystal blue eyes were shadowed. "You know what you did," she said obscurely.

He sighed. Women. "I apologized for that. I'm trying to pretend it never happened."

"Not that! I mean last night."

73

He stared blankly at her. "What?"

She paused, looking down at her wine. "You told everyone you're finding guys for me to go out with."

Oh, shit. That. Yeah, she'd looked kind of hurt. He'd just been trying to joke around and tease like they always did.

"Damn, Kerri, I'm sorry. But you never told me it was a big secret."

"It's embarrassing," she said in a small voice, not looking at him.

"I'm sorry." Damn, he was apologizing a lot lately. His beer arrived and he picked it up.

He had the feeling that wasn't all there was to her frostiness, but he really didn't want to start talking about "the kiss" right now. Kerri moved over to talk to Sela, Hailey and Miguel standing in a group along with a man Mitch recognized. He followed and joined them.

"How are Hailey and Miguel feeling today?" Mitch asked.

"We're fine," they answered as one. Then Hailey asked, "Why'd you leave so early?"

"It wasn't early. You guys were out late."

"Hi, Mitch." The other man in the group spoke up and held out a hand.

"Jack." Mitch shook his hand firmly. "Hey, how are you?"

"Really well, thanks." Jack was a client whose divorce had recently been finalized. It had been messy and Mitch had felt sorry for the poor guy. His wife had tried to take him for every penny she could and had fought an ugly custody-battle for the children. She'd even fought over the dog. "How about you? Life is easier now?"

"Hell of a lot easier," Jack said wholeheartedly. "Thank God that chapter of my life is over with."

Mitch nodded sympathetically. "Yeah, I know. Glad things worked out okay for you. Jack, do you know Kerri?

She's the owner of the yoga part of White Lotus. Kerri, this is Jack Farnham, one of my clients."

Kerri reached out and shook his hand. "Pleased to meet you."

Jack smiled at her admiringly. "Recently divorced. Nice to meet you too."

Shit. Mitch scowled. Kerri did *not* want to get messed up with this guy and all the baggage he carried around, not to mention a vicious, greedy ex-wife and three children whose custody had been a major battle. But Kerri was smiling at the guy.

"You don't look like the typical spa customer." She fluttered her long eyelashes at him.

He grinned. "I actually come every week for a manicure and a massage. Amanda is the best massage therapist I've ever had."

Mitch's frown deepened.

Kerri nodded. "Yes, she's great. Has she tried her new massage oil on you?"

"No...I don't think so."

Kerri pursed her lips thoughtfully. "Probably too feminine a fragrance for you. You'll have to check with her about some of the other oils she has."

Mitch wrinkled his forehead. What the hell was she talking about? Oils?

"So." Jack turned to Mitch. "I hear you're trying some different things in your divorce work."

"Like what?" Kerri looked from Jack to Mitch, brows raised.

Mitch sighed. "I've been doing more and more dispute resolution work for couples that are divorcing."

"Oh. But do they still get divorced?"

He laughed. "Well, yeah. I'm not a marriage counselor. I was getting frustrated at all the animosity and ugliness, so I started trying some conflict resolution stuff to help them work things out. Not resolve their marital issues, although I have to say it has happened a couple of times. Mostly I just try to help work out how to divide assets, custody, stuff like that."

"Oh. That's what you were talking to my dad about last weekend."

He nodded.

"I know you were getting a reputation as someone who could work any kind of deal out, no matter how bitter the couple was. So you're actually doing more of that."

He nodded again, her words warming him, and she met his eyes.

"Wow," she said. "That's really different for you. I thought all lawyers wanted to drag things out as long as possible so they could make as much money as they could."

He let his breath out in a deflated whoosh. "You have such a high opinion of me."

"So, what would be your advice to couples?" Jack asked. "Litigation? Mediation?"

"My advice would be to not get married," Mitch said dryly, and everybody laughed. "Seriously. If they could only hear the horror stories of the hatred and destruction divorcing couples inflict on each other, they might think twice about getting married. They think they love each other and they don't believe that in a few years, they'll be emotionally and physically beating each other up, spending thousands of dollars fighting over a five-hundred-dollar painting or a dog, or accusing the other of child molestation or being a drunken slut."

He felt Kerri's eyes on him and glanced at her. She'd heard this stuff before, no surprise to her.

But her eyes flashed and the corners of her mouth tipped down. "You're so cynical. You shouldn't be talking like that in front of Hailey and Miguel. They're getting married in two weeks. We should all be happy for them. So listen. Why does California have the most lawyers in the country while New Jersey has the most toxic waste sites?" She waited a beat.

No, Kerri, not now. He sighed inwardly.

"New Jersey got first choice."

Everyone laughed.

"What's the difference between lawyers and accountants?"

The others all grinned. "At least accountants *know* they're boring."

They laughed again, except Mitch, who grimaced.

She looked at him, shaking her head, a little smile playing on her pretty mouth. "What's wrong with lawyer jokes?" She paused. "Lawyers don't think they're funny and no one else thinks they're jokes."

More laughter followed, and now Mitch shook his head, trying to be a good sport, but damn, these lawyer jokes were getting to him. It was fine when he knew she was just teasing him, but lately she'd been so cool to him it was tough to take it in a light-hearted vein. Sparks shot between them as they exchanged a glare.

"Would you two just stop it!" Hailey burst out.

The group grew quiet. Kerri and Mitch both looked at her, startled.

"Uh...stop what?" Kerri glanced at Mitch.

"What is with you two?" Hailey looked from one to the other. "Last night you two just kept at each other, pushing each other's buttons, and tonight it's even worse."

"That's how we talk to each other," Kerri said in a small voice. "We like to tease each other."

"There's teasing and then there's tormenting. I don't get it. What's going on?"

They were both silent, again glancing at each other.

"Nothing," Mitch said finally. "Kerri, I think Sela and your parents are trying to get your attention."

She looked across the room where they beckoned her over. "Excuse me." She flashed an apologetic smile at Jack then separated from the group and went over to talk to their parents.

Hailey and Miguel also excused themselves.

"Wow," Jack said under his breath as he and Mitch both watched Kerri walk away, the straps criss-crossing her smooth bare back, hips swaying under the filmy black skirt. "She's hot. She single?"

Kerri would kill him, but... "She is, but she's kind of flaky," he told Jack. "Not your type at all."

10

Hailey caught up to Kerri and grabbed her arm.
"Like, what is the deal with you and Mitch?" she challenged Kerri. "You guys are our friends. Everybody noticed you two going at each other last night."

Kerri swallowed, her throat tight. "It's complicated."

Hailey nodded, slowly released her arm but gave her hand a squeeze. "Okay. But if you want to talk about it at all, I'm here."

Kerri just nodded. She couldn't talk about this. She didn't even understand herself what was going on. That kiss had messed everything up, and much as she tried to pretend it had never happened, everything was different now. It was like seeing the world through different eyes.

She looked around and found Mitch across the room still talking to Jack, but watching her. Her belly did a flip flop, and she slowly turned and walked over to her parents where Sela had joined them.

"Hi, Kerri." Her dad gave her a brief hug. "We were just telling Sela what a great party this is. The place looks awesome." He smiled at his eldest daughter. "You've done a great job, honey."

A corner of Kerri's mouth turned down. Yeah, *Sela* had done a great job. The few things she'd allowed Kerri to help with were insignificant. The fact that Kerri, too, had a successful business was once again overlooked. She forced a smile as Sela's two teenage daughters joined them, looking startlingly grown up in their fancy dresses and makeup.

"You two look very sophisticated tonight," she told them, giving them big hugs, which they returned. "Are you enjoying the party?"

"It's cool, Aunt Kerri! And I love your yoga studio," Claire said.

"Thank you."

Sela's husband, Doug, appeared and wrapped his arm around his wife. "I don't know how you do it." He smiled at her with admiration as Sela reached out to smooth a lock of hair off her younger daughter's cheek.

Sela's daughter Jasmine snorted. "Dad! Last night you told her she was a controlling b—"

"Oh, Jasmine, never mind that." Sela gave a light laugh. "Why don't you and Claire go find your brother?"

"But—" Jasmine started to protest, but Sela was shepherding everyone across the room for an impromptu tour.

Kerri watched them disappear, leaving her alone. She could have gone with them, but all the fun had been sucked out of the evening. She sighed. Much as she wished she could just leave, she was stuck there for the duration.

Time for another glass of wine.

As she waited for her drink, Mitch appeared beside her. He leaned his elbows on the bar, beer bottle clasped between his hands, head bowed. "Are you having fun?"

She sighed. "No."

"Me neither." He turned his head to look at her. "I hate this, Kerri."

Her heart tightened painfully. "Me, too."

"What do I have to do to fix things? Just tell me."

She tilted her head up to look at him, and laughed humorlessly. "Hell if I know."

He slid an arm around her, hand on her waist, and pulled her closer to his side.

She tried to pull away. "I don't think this is going to fix things." He pulled her back. "Seriously, Mitch."

"What?" he murmured.

She stepped away from him, but it was difficult. Heat flared in her at his touch. His hand drifted across her back and found bare skin where her dress was cut low, sending shivers through her that were not unpleasant. Her breasts felt full and heavy and her heart pumped wildly. She bit back a moan.

"Tell me, Kerri," he murmured, again pulling her closer.

This time she softened, savored the warmth of his body, the comfort of feeling someone big and strong close to her. Oh, no. No, no, no. "Tell you what?"

"How to fix things. How to fix us. 'Cause I don't have a hot clue. I know I screwed up, but I apologized and I've been trying to act like it never happened."

"You act like you hate me," she whispered, staring at the glass of wine in front of her.

"God, no! Of course I don't hate you. You're the one who's acting like *you* hate *me*."

"Should we fight over that, too?" Humor tugged the corners of her mouth as she lifted her eyes to his. He smiled and his amber eyes were warm as they turned to face each other, bodies brushing together. Electricity sizzled and their eyes joined like lasers, each of them unable to look away. Again, her breasts swelled, nipples tingling agonizingly, and she melted, a slow liquid heat deep inside her. Her lips parted a little and when his eyes dropped to her mouth, she grew hotter. Her mouth actually watered, wanting to open and feel his mouth on hers, his tongue inside her.

"We can't do this," she whispered, fighting the sensations swirling through her, trying to be sensible.

"Maybe this is how we fix things," he murmured, gaze still locked on her mouth.

She shook her head. "No," she choked out. "We're just making things worse."

Suddenly, they both became aware they were in a crowded room. Kerri glanced around and damned if Miguel and Hailey weren't across the room, watching them stand there as if they were about to kiss.

Kerri pulled back out of his arms. "I-I'm going to the ladies' room." She rushed out of the room. In the hallway, she ignored people she knew and bolted into changing room at the end of the hall. In a bathroom stall, she sat there, her face in her hands, trying to get control of herself.

What the hell was all that? Her mind was a twisted mass of confused emotions and thoughts. It had felt so good and so right to be in Mitch's arms, and when he looked at her like that, warm and attentive, it made her feel so special. Like before, when they were friends. Okay, maybe not quite like before. She'd never felt quite like this before. Ever.

What on earth was happening? Mitch had been coming on to her again, and—she had to admit it—she loved it. She wanted him on her side again, not fighting with her like they had been. She wanted him to look at her like that again, not coldly or angrily, like he had been for the last week, but warmly. And, stunningly, she wanted to press herself against his big, hard body, rub against him...God!

She shoved her hair back and sat up straight. She stared up at the ceiling.

The door opened and laughing voices entered. She recognized Hailey and Sela. Apparently they were unaware of her in the end stall.

"What is with Kerri and Mitch?" Sela asked. "Did you talk to her?"

"I tried. Something's going on. You should have heard them! They're both as tense as cats in a canoe. But she wouldn't say much." Hailey sighed. "I wish they'd just get it over with. Everyone knows they're crazy about each other. Except them."

"Yeah. They're so cute together. Except lately. I was afraid knives were going to come out or something."

Their voices faded as the heavy washroom door closed behind them.

Kerri sat there for long moments. They were insane! She and Mitch were not crazy about each other. They were *friends.*

ClllllO

Mitch stood there after Kerri bolted to the washroom. Shit. She was panicked and he didn't blame her. He was terrified, too. Man, what was he thinking? Hell, he wasn't thinking. Not with his big head, anyway.

No, blaming this on hormones wasn't right. If he was just horny, he could have lots of girls. That had never been a problem for him. But he didn't want any other girls. He was hot for Kerri.

Shame and embarrassment slid over him and he rubbed his face. He glanced around the room, but everyone was busy laughing and talking.

How could he have done that to his best friend? No wonder she was pissed at him. He took a deep breath.

And yet...he'd felt her response. Yeah, she'd tried to pull away, tried to pretend nothing was happening, but he'd *felt* it. Just like he'd felt it that afternoon when he'd kissed her. He took the blame for that, for initiating it, for acting like a sex-starved teenager, but there was no denying she had kissed him back. *Really* kissed him back. She'd melted under him, held on to him, opened for him.

Jesus, he was getting hard again just thinking about it. Great. He shifted from one foot to the other. Then Hailey and Sela walked into the room, talking seriously about something. They both looked at him, then away.

Shit. They were talking about him. And since they were women, they, too, were probably pissed off at him for coming on to Kerri. He groaned. He needed another beer.

After he'd been to the bar, stopped by several people on the way to talk, there was still no sign of Kerri. He checked his watch. It had been a while since she'd taken off.

He wandered out into the hall, casually looking for her, but no luck. He stood at the door of her office, thinking she might have ducked out of the party for a few moments of peace and quiet. He poked his head in the door. Someone was in there, in the dark... Kerri? He started to speak, then realized a man and woman were locked in a heated embrace. What the fuck? A hot wave of jealousy rushed over him.

Ah hell. It was Kerri's parents.

He stood there for few seconds, grinning, light with relief and amusement. Whoa. Forty years of marriage and still hot for each other. He shook his head as he silently backed out of the room. Amazing. It was almost enough to make him rethink his feelings about marriage. Almost.

Mitch returned to the party, wandered over to one of the armchairs that had been pushed to the perimeter of the room, and threw himself into it. From there he spotted Kerri. He watched her talk and laugh animatedly for a few minutes until she excused herself and left the room.

This time he followed her into her darkened yoga studio. He watched her stroll slowly through it, stopping in the middle of the room to remove those killer high heels. Then she continued toward her office, shoes dangling from her fingertips.

He wondered if her parents were still making out in her office. Better stop her before she busted in on them.

"Hey," he called softly.

She turned. "Mitch."

She gazed at him, her eyes huge, questioning, fearful. They stared at each other for long, silent, heart-thumping moments.

He took a step toward her. She moved toward him. And then she was in his arms, and he wasn't sure if she'd come to him or he'd gone to her, but their bodies were pressed together.

11

The shoes clunked to the floor and he kissed her. Hot, open-mouthed kisses, bending her back over one arm, the other fisted in her hair, and yes, thank Christ, she was kissing him back. Her small hands gripped his shoulders as if she was drowning and she opened for him, her tongue stroking his as he licked into her mouth.

He couldn't get her close enough, wanted to be inside her, wanted to not just taste her but devour her. He panted as he lifted his mouth and tilted his head for a deeper angle and kissed her again with all the pent-up frustration he'd felt over the last few weeks.

He pushed the tiny straps of her dress off her shoulders with his fingertips, laid a soft lingering kiss there and breathed in the scent of her. "God, you smell good. What is that?"

"Ylang-ylang." Her fingers dug into his shoulders.

What? Never mind. His hands slid lower, over the silky black fabric covering her breasts, and the soft flesh filled his hands with such perfection all the air rushed out of his lungs.

She moaned, breasts swelling into his hands, and her intense response made him ache to have her. He gently, slowly, pushed the fabric aside, baring her breasts, and his heart stopped as he looked down at her. Christ Jesus, she was beautiful.

He was so hard it hurt, so overcome with the incredible reality of holding her in his arms, touching her like this, he almost came. He buried his face against her, gulping for air, whole body tense.

Her arms slid around him and held him tightly against her while they both struggled to breath.

"This is insane," Kerri gasped.

He inhaled deeply against her skin, drawing in her delicious scent. "I know." Eyes closed, he focused on breathing and control. His body vibrated with blistering need and excitement. She trembled against him, and his fingers tightened on her breasts. Stiff little nipples rubbed against his palms and fire burned in his belly, heat sizzled over his skin.

"I'm not taking the blame for this one," he finally said in a strangled voice. "You want this too."

"No."

He drew back, anger rising in him again. "Yes, you do. Admit it, Kerri. I can feel you respond to me."

She gazed back at him, her brows drawn down, lips trembling.

"Tell me," he ground out.

"Yes." Her eyes fell closed. "Okay, yes, dammit! I want you too. It's crazy but I can't help it."

Thank Christ.

"Then there's no problem," he murmured, lowering his face to her hair. He kissed the silky strands, rubbed his face against them and inhaled again, loving the spicy floral scent of her hair.

"Yes, there is a problem." Her voice wobbled. "There's a freaking *huge* problem. What about our friendship?"

"I'm feeling very friendly right now," he assured her, face still buried in her hair, hands still stroking her soft lushness.

"Oh God, I can't believe this is happening."

His hands stilled. He wanted to push the dress all the way off her body and feel her skin, see all of her. But he didn't want to go too far, too fast. He didn't want to be the bad guy here. Again. He lifted his head and very carefully drew the little straps of her dress back onto her shoulders.

She stood in his arms, teeth sunk into her swollen bottom lip, eyes huge and smoky blue. She looked so incredibly sexy it took every ounce of restraint he possessed to lean away from her. "I guess we should talk." Talking about feelings was not his favorite thing to do—especially with a raging hard-on—but seemed necessary.

Kerri appeared to be having some trouble breathing, her high, round breasts rising and falling quickly, enticingly, under her dress. "I guess so," she whispered. "But not here."

"Okay." He waited.

"My place. After the party."

"How'd you get here?"

"I got a ride with Sela and Doug."

Perfect. "I'll drive you home, then."

She nodded, still staring up at him with unfocused, dilated eyes. He smoothed her dress over her waist and hips, stepped back and picked up her shoes. He handed them to her, walking with her out of the room. At the door, they paused and she held his arm while she lifted one foot to put on her shoe, then the other. Then, smoothing her hair back, she sucked in a deep breath and they returned to the party.

⟅⟆

Kerri's mind buzzed, a churning jumble of confusion. She pasted a smile on as she talked to her guests, said good night to those who were leaving. When the last person had left, she and Sela gave each other a weary high-five.

"Awesome party, Sela. You did a great job."

"Thanks. You made quite an impression tonight. All my customers were asking about you. I think you can expect some new clients."

"Oh. Wow. That's great." Sela was complimenting her? Holy crap.

Then Kerri remembered Mitch was waiting for her, and she couldn't get out of there fast enough. "I'll talk to you more tomorrow."

Mitch waited for her at the front door and set his hand on the small of her back as they walked to his vehicle. Warmth radiated from his fingers through her body.

"I walked in on your parents," Mitch told her as they drove to her place. "They were getting busy in your office."

"Huh?" Her mind twirled with thoughts of Mitch's hands on her breasts and his mouth on hers, her body tingled, and she had no clue what he was talking about.

He grinned. "They were kissing. Pretty hot too, for an old couple. I walked in on them, but luckily they didn't see me."

"Oh dear lord."

He laughed. "Hey, it's a good thing. Your parents are amazing. I can't believe they're still doing that after forty years."

"Yeah. I guess." Mitch was right, it was better that than the alternative.

That only diverted her temporarily, however, from the kiss she and Mitch had shared. Excitement clutched at her stomach and her head spun as they drove to her place. What on earth was happening here? This was so crazy.

12

Once in her condo, they stood in her living room for several heartbeats, looking at each other. She ached for him, burning with a breathless, throbbing need.

"I don't want to talk," she breathed, moving toward him.

"Oh, thank Christ." He scooped her up and carried her down the hall.

Once in her bedroom, he let her slide down his body until her feet touched the floor. She stepped out of her shoes, wound her arms around his neck and kissed him.

His mouth was firm at first, then opened for her and he kissed her back, open-mouthed, deeply, wetly. His hands came to her waist, and then they were all over each other, going at each other with long, desperate kisses.

She tugged on his tie until it came loose then went to work on the buttons of his shirt. Heat radiated off him, his shirt damp and warm beneath her hands. She bent and pressed her open mouth to his chest as she bared it.

She'd seen his chest before, of course. Many times. And in fact, she'd admired it. Smooth, broad muscles tapered down to his six pack abs. But now...she was seeing it in a whole new way, now she got to touch it, kiss it, inhale it, as she pressed her mouth there.

He drew in a sharp, audible breath as she kissed and licked her way lower, hands tugging his shirt out of his pants. She undid the buckle of his belt, loosened it and opened the fastener at top of the zipper. His hands covered hers and stopped her.

She glanced up at him, biting her lip. "What? Is this…weird?"

"Weird? No, I definitely wouldn't say weird."

"I just mean because we've known each other so long…"

He smiled, his eyes so hot they scorched her. "Not weird at all," he said softly. "I just want to slow down a little."

She smiled back. His palms skimmed over her shoulders, sending hot shivers through her, and he pushed the straps of her dress down over her arms, further and further until the bodice of the dress dropped to her waist. Breasts bared, nipples tight and tingling, she watched his face as he looked at her, and so badly wanted him to like what he saw. And then…she knew he did, as his eyes darkened, his jaw tightened and his hands came up to gently cup her breasts.

"God, Kerri, you're gorgeous," he said hoarsely.

A small moan escaped her.

His palms rubbed over her nipples, and she shuddered under his touch, pleasure cascading over her. Her lower tummy was a hot ache of desire, warm liquid need pulsing between her legs, and her inner muscles clenched hard with yearning.

He kissed her again, a slow meeting of their mouths, and his tongue brushed her bottom lip as the kiss ended. Heat trickled through her. She drew back and their eyes met again. Eyelids heavy, her eyes drifted shut as she leaned into him for another kiss. She needed more, more of him — his mouth, his tongue, his touch. He licked again, licked into her mouth, and she opened wider for him, sucked on him.

Her dress crumpled around her waist and she pushed

the sides of his shirt apart, then wound her arms around his neck and pressed her aching breasts against his hard chest, skin to scorching skin. His arms tightened around her and the kiss grew hotter. Frantic whimpers of pleasure and panting breaths filled the quiet room.

He gently stroked up her bare back, took her face in his hands and held her while he lifted his mouth from hers, changed the angle, then took her mouth again in a searing kiss. God, they were both going to go up in flames. His fingers burned her face, his shoulders and neck almost feverish to her touch.

He leaned his forehead on hers, panting for breath. "Jesus," he gasped.

She laid her hands over his, still on her face, and they stood like that for long, throbbing moments. Her heart raced with a frantic beat and every nerve ending jumped and quivered with urgent need.

He clicked on the lamp beside the bed and she met his eyes as she shimmied her dress over her hips and let it fall to the floor in a small black puddle of silk, leaving her in lacy black cheekie panties that barely covering anything.

He watched her intently as she shed her dress, his eyes warm with appreciation. A thrill zapped through her that she pleased him.

He stripped his shirt off his shoulders, tossed it aside, and the sight of his naked torso forced all the air out of her lungs. God, he was beautiful.

He toed out of his dress shoes, then unzipped his pants with an efficient tug, and shed socks along with the pants. Snug black boxer briefs barely contained his massive erection and Kerri studied him with admiration.

Now this was Mitch as she'd never seen him. He was a gorgeous guy, but she'd never given the size of his package much thought before. Now...wow. Her mouth actually watered. She wanted to see all of him. She wanted to taste him.

She crossed the short distance between them to stroke her hands down his smooth chest and defined abs, his lean hips, the bones square and strong under her hands. She tipped her head back to look at him.

"Are you sure, Kerri?" he asked softly. "I don't want you to be mad at me for pushing you into doing something you don't want to."

"I'm sure." She met his eyes. Their gazes held, the air thick and hot and heavy around them, and she swallowed. "I am *so* sure. If we don't do this, I'm going to die."

"God, me too." He picked her up and deposited her on the bed. He came down beside her, his heavy weight tipping the mattress so she rolled into him. She flung one leg over his hip, arched her pelvis into him, only thin layers of cotton and lace between them. She grabbed the thick muscles of his upper arm with one hand, slid the other under him, so she could get closer.

But even as he took her mouth again, he pushed her away, onto her back on the mattress. He left her mouth and nibbled his way down her neck to her shoulder, then lower. Her breasts lifted, full and tight, in anticipation of his touch. He kissed her clavicle, the top of one breast, and then the other.

She moaned in helpless excitement, and when he finally licked one nipple, sweet hot pleasure rushed through her. He slowly licked again with a hot, velvet tongue and she whimpered. Then his mouth closed over her and it was exquisite...astonishingly beautiful. When he sucked and tugged on her sensitive flesh, her eyes rolled back in her head, pulls of ecstasy shooting from nipple to womb.

"You taste so sweet," he muttered. "Such pretty breasts."

Again, she arched against him, hips lifting, pleading, inviting, as he sucked and pulled on her tender nipples. He cupped her breasts, lifting her nipples to his mouth, one, then the other, and she thought she might die from the pleasure. Her head rolled back and forth on the mattress, mindless with rapture.

He pressed his mouth between her breasts, then lower across her tummy, sending more shivers of delight through her.

"Tell me again what that fragrance is." His nose rested below her belly button and he inhaled deeply.

"Ylang-ylang. It's the flower of the...um...cananga tree." She could barely speak as his mouth slid lower. "In Indonesia, ylang-ylang flowers are spread on the bed of newlywed couples. It's..." He pressed a kiss onto her hip bone just above the black lace. "It's an..." He hooked his fingers into the panties and tugged them down. "...an aphrodisiac. Oh!" She lifted her hips and he whisked her panties over her legs and off.

Hot, hard hands pushed her thighs apart as he moved over her.

"God, I want to taste you," he muttered, voice thick, and her belly flip-flopped at his words. Her thighs quivered and she ached there, knew she was wet for him.

His fingers parted her folds and stroked through and yes, she was wet, so wet.

For a moment she couldn't believe this was happening. This was *Mitch* touching her like this, so intimately, so arousingly. She should be uncomfortable, embarrassed...but all she was, was unbearably excited. She let herself go, breathing a sigh of relief at finally giving in to the sexual tension she could now admit had been building between her and Mitch for weeks. She floated on a cloud of erotic sensation as he licked her, kissed her swollen folds, then found her clit and sucked softly.

She cried out, fisted her hands in the duvet they were still laying atop, head twisting from side to side as pleasure built and spiraled inside her.

"Oh, that's so good."

He found the exact spot she needed him to stroke and he pressed his tongue and lips expertly against her as he took her higher, flying, exploding in a shower of glitter and brilliant light, exquisite pleasure tearing through her in a blinding orgasm.

CXXXXO

Kerri still trembled moments later as Mitch moved up beside her on the bed. Her eyes were closed as he leaned over and kissed her mouth, and she barely kissed him back. Her shaking hands came up to clutch his biceps and her mouth opened then closed.

He marveled at her responsiveness, her incredible sensitivity, how hard she'd come in his mouth. Masculine pride, along with awe, appreciation and gratification at his incredible good fortune of having her—finally—swelled inside him.

Since the day he'd kissed her after helping her move to her new studio, she'd been in his thoughts and fantasies constantly. It had driven him crazy as he fought against the feelings he was having for her, wild with wanting her, infuriated that he could even think such things. His erotic dreams, full of images of kissing her, touching her, tasting her, turned into sweaty, gut-twisting nightmares of her with all those other guys she'd been dating.

"Are you okay?" He smoothed her hair off her face. She turned her head into his hand and kissed his palm and his hand stilled there. His heart lurched to a stop in his chest. Jesus. He was done.

"No," she murmured. "I think I'm unconscious."

He smiled, then frowned. He needed his wallet. He rolled off her and onto the floor, dragged his wrinkled pants over and fumbled in the pocket until he found what he needed.

When he returned to her she looked at him questioningly and he held up the little package.

"Oh." She gave a small smile.

He ripped it open and rolled the condom onto his throbbing cock, fumbling a bit in his high excitement.

He tried to swallow through an obstruction in his throat, his face hot. He moved between her legs, nudged her thighs apart with his knee, held his weight off her on his elbows, and paused.

"Yes," she whispered. Her hands came up to clutch his body, slid down his sides to his hips and pulled him forward. She took him in one hand and stroked him, pulling down. He swelled uncontrollably, painfully. She shifted her hips and raised her knees, directing the head of his penis into her soft, wet heat.

He nudged into the warm, wet velvet of her sex. Tight and hot around his cock, she squeezed him inside her, pulling him in with her muscles. Jesus! How did she do that? The sensations were incredibly erotic, pleasure slamming from his groin to his toes, making him feel weak yet powerful, hard yet soft.

"All the way," she urged him, tipping her hips even more, hands on his ass, pulling him into her. "I want you inside me. All of you."

Her words inflamed him, scorched away his self-control, and he thrust into her hard, filling her all the way, the head of his shaft pressing against her womb and she shuddered beneath him, still urging him on with hands and inner muscles and whimpered pleas.

They came together as if they had wanted this, waited for this, forever. It felt right. It felt perfect.

He paused a moment, struggling for breath and control, his balls tight. He looked down at her and she opened her eyes at that exact moment. Satisfaction and pleasure darkened her blue eyes and her gaze caught his and trapped it. The moment seemed to freeze in time.

The pressure at the base of his spine exploded. He drew out and thrust in, again and again, lost, frantic, his urgent hunger for her desperately seeking satiety. Her eyes fell closed again, and he hid his face in her fragrant neck as he buried himself in her again and again, feeling the bite of her nails on his shoulders as she clutched him.

Pleasure roared through him and he poured himself into her, hot, reckless, groaning against her neck as he pulsed through an intense orgasm.

When the draining shudders ended, he carefully lowered himself onto her, taking some weight on his elbows so as not to crush her. Her hands moved over his back, damp with sweat. "God, Kerri," was all he could say. She'd blown his fucking mind.

"Mmmm."

They lay together, silent but for rasping breaths and pounding hearts. Then he turned his face to her neck and pressed a kiss to the soft skin there, breathing in her warm scent.

He rolled to his back, taking her with him, wanting to stay inside her. He was still semi-hard despite the heart-stopping orgasm he had just experienced. Christ, he felt like he'd been run over by a truck, yet he wanted more.

Kerri snuggled against him, her face on his chest, and he tightened his arms around her. A moment later her breathing slowed and, lifting his head, he could see she was asleep. He smiled wryly. Girls weren't supposed to fall asleep after sex.

He stroked her hair, enjoying the feel of her body against his, her smooth legs twined with his, her silky hair, her warm breath on his chest. Oh man. Why had they waited so long?

He let out a long slow breath, his gut clenching in realization of what they'd done. Not that he regretted it. God, that had been the best sex of his life.

But now what was going to happen to them?

13

Mitch had barely left Sunday afternoon when Liam called to arrange their dinner date that evening. Kerri was distinctly unenthusiastic about seeing him after what had just happened. But she and Mitch hadn't had that talk they were going to, and she didn't know exactly what had just happened. There had been no words of love or commitment, and she wasn't sure she wanted that anyway. It was Mitch.

She had no idea what was going on between them. Sure, he'd left her with a warm kiss on the mouth and a hand sliding caressingly over her butt, but what did that mean?

They were friends. Now they were friends with benefits. She grimaced at the expression she hated. What else to call it? Fuck buddies? Was that what they were now?

So she found herself agreeing to meet Liam at seven for dinner.

She glanced at her watch and had to get moving to get to the spa. She'd arranged to meet someone there that afternoon, while the spa was closed, one of her clients who was a photographer. In exchange for some free yoga classes, Neta had agreed to take some pictures to put on the website. Despite Sela's assertion that they needed a professional, Kerri had decided to try her hand at working on it. Although she knew she could do it, she also knew that taking professional-quality digital photographs was beyond her talents.

She tried to make sense of what had happened the night before as she drove to the spa. Admittedly it had been a while since she'd even been on a date, prior to Mitch's help, let alone had sex. Maybe this was what happened when you went too long without. Anyone would do.

Unfortunately, it didn't seem to be a situation where any man would do. Mitch was the only one who did it for her. In fact, Mitch was the one who made her that horny. She'd been perfectly happy in her celibate world before this all started. Sad, but true.

She'd have to study up on tantric sex and sexual continence. Wasn't it supposed to be good for you to go without orgasms? Supposedly improve your immune system or something like that.

Like that was possible. With Mitch, she needed an orgasm like she needed oxygen. Even more, she needed to give *him* an orgasm. That melting sensation in her womb drizzled through her again and she sighed.

"I'll need to light it properly," Neta said as they wandered around. "Sunday is probably the best day, as you're closed."

"Yes," Kerri said. "Can you do it next Sunday?"

"Sure. I'll bring all my gear. I'll shoot lots and you can decide which ones you want to use."

"Excellent."

CINE

Liam lifted a casual hand when he spotted her across the restaurant. Kerri smiled at the hostess and made her way over to the table where he sat.

"Hi!" She took the hand he extended. To her surprise,

he pulled her in and kissed her cheek. She sat down at the small table. "How are you?"

"I'm great." His eyes moved over her like it was the first time he'd seen her. "You?"

"Very well, thank you."

"How was the party last night?"

"It went really well. I was exhausted, but it was good. Tons of people came, lots of clients and maybe some new ones. It was really nice to feel all the support from our family and friends and clients for this new spa."

"You must love your work. How many classes do you teach in a week?"

"Well, right now I'm doing three or four classes a day except Sunday. I'm just hiring some new instructors. I want to expand how many classes I offer and maybe offer some different types of classes, so I definitely need some help. I have other ideas of things I want to expand into as well."

"Wow. You must be in great shape doing that many classes."

She laughed again and shrugged.

The waitress came and took orders for drinks. They ordered dinner, ate, engaged in some interesting conversation. Liam seemed nice—intelligent, sensitive, maybe a little cynical and jaded. But after the things he'd seen and done, who could blame him.

The evening passed pleasantly and Kerri always enjoyed getting to know someone new, but she found herself feeling...bored. Restless. Wishing for a little sizzle, a little excitement.

Like with Mitch.

Heat flared low in her core.

She shouldn't have gone on this date. She had absolutely no interest in seeing Liam again, even if he wanted to. Unbelievably, he was the first guy Mitch had set her up with who seemed normal and nice—actual husband potential. And she couldn't care less.

Liam didn't seem to feel the same, though, and when they left the restaurant he invited her out again. She didn't know what to do. She had no idea what was going on with her and Mitch other than hot sex. So she asked him to call her closer to the weekend.

He kissed her cheek again after walking her to her car, very sweet but completely bland.

⟨⟩))✿((⟨⟩

After her Monday morning class had emptied, Kerri wandered into the spa and found Sela in her office.

"So, did you recover from the party?" Sela looked up at Kerri. "Holy shit. Are you okay?"

"What?" Nervously, Kerri put a hand to her hair.

"You look...I don't know. Different."

"Bah." Kerri waved a hand dismissively. "I just had a really good class."

Sela was still looking at her strangely.

"So, the party went well," Kerri said. "All your planning paid off."

Sela nodded and smiled with satisfaction. "Yes, I thought it went well. Lots of high-profile clients came. It's good for getting word out about the new spa. Hopefully it will spark some interest, maybe bring in some new clients."

Kerri nodded enthusiastically. "Definitely."

"So what's up for you today?"

"I'm working on hiring some new instructors. I'm adding new classes, but I'm pretty much maxed out. I know some girls who are interested in teaching, so we're going to talk."

Sela frowned. "Don't you have a structured interview process? How will you know if they're qualified? Or suited to the job?"

Kerri grinned. "I'll just know. Trust my instincts."

Sela's frown deepened. "You can't run a business on instincts, Kerri. What—"

Kerri interrupted, losing her patience a bit. "I've been doing okay so far, Sela. Just because I'm leasing space from you doesn't give you the right to tell me how to run my business."

Silence expanded between them, then Sela held up her hands and leaned back in her chair. "You're right. But it also doesn't give you the right to try to tell *me* how to run *my* spa. Or how to decorate it so the 'energy flows'."

Kerri's chest tightened. She couldn't believe Sela had said that. She'd just been trying to help. And she knew what she was talking about. "It's not exactly the same," she said slowly. "The reception and waiting area are where *my* clients come, too. I want the atmosphere to be warm and welcoming for them."

They just looked at each other, and then Kerri shrugged and turned and left. Sela was so dominating, always the big sister. Even though Kerri knew she should stand up to her, her mind went empty when she had to argue with Sela. It had always been like that.

This arrangement wasn't going to be as easy as she'd thought. Sela's offer had initially seemed heaven-sent, coming at the exact moment she needed help. She'd been having such a hard time finding appropriate commercial space for her studio when her lease had been cancelled, she'd almost thought she was going to lose her business. But when Sela had made the proposal, Kerri had never anticipated conflict between them.

She should have known, though. It was always like this between them. She could never measure up to Sela's perfection—in Sela's eyes or in their family's. Or even Mitch's eyes when it came to business, apparently.

Mitch had just finished a Monday morning meeting with another collaborative lawyer and a couple who were divorcing, curiously amicably. He was happy about that though, because his mind wasn't fully functional. He was having a hard time getting Kerri *out* of his head and the law *in*.

So what were the rules in a situation like this? If it had been any other girl, he would have already called. But it was Kerri. They didn't talk every day. Sometimes a week would go by without them talking, although they almost always saw each other on weekends when they got together with friends.

Should he call her? What would he say? Christ, this was stupid.

He was completely blown away by how sexy Kerri was. They'd been friends for so long, and he knew she was attractive, but over the years he hadn't pictured her in bed like he had in the last few weeks. Who knew she was so hot?

God, he was getting hard again thinking about her. The way she'd responded to him like he was hottest thing going, the way he'd made her come so hard. So many times. Jesus. It was all he could do to stop himself from getting up and leaving work to go find her. He'd do her in the middle of her yoga studio if he could.

Which thought led his dirty mind to another: how much impact did her yoga have on those muscles of hers? She could squeeze him like a fist when he was inside her. It was insane.

Maybe she knew some kind of tantric secret. Oh man. Now he was really hot, and he had another client meeting in five minutes. A good workout at lunch time would help.

He called Garth Layton back, the lawyer who'd approached him about reopening the custody agreement for Mariah and Bob Sinclair.

"I talked to her on Friday," he told Garth. "And exactly

as I thought, she totally rejected the idea. There's no way in hell she'll let him have the kid for her birthday this year."

"He's willing to go back into court to fight for this," Garth warned him.

Mitch sighed. "Yeah, I figured that. I told her that was a distinct possibility. She's willing to take the chance of having to go through that again." He didn't mention to the other attorney the fact that the legal system was slow enough that they wouldn't even have a court date until well past the girl's birthday. Especially if Mitch took his time with things. His gut clenched again.

"You'll hear back from me," Garth promised.

After hanging up, Mitch really wanted to talk to Kerri. She'd always been the one he could talk to about pretty much anything. Enough of not seeming too eager. He was fucking desperate.

"Hey!" She sounded pleased to hear from him. "How are you?"

"Really busy. But okay. You?"

"Yeah, busy. I've been talking to some girls about instructing, so I can offer more classes."

"Really? You're going to give up teaching?"

"Of course not!" She laughed, recognized his teasing. "I just can't do any more. Part of my plan with this move was to expand, take advantage of the new location."

"Why don't you tell me all about it tonight?"

"Tonight?"

"Yeah. Let's go out. Drinks...dinner? What would you like to do?"

"Um...I was just out last night. How about I cook dinner at my place?"

"Even better," he said fervently. "What time?"

"Six?"

"See you then."

After work, he went home and changed out of his suit

and tie into a pair of baggy cargo pants and old UCSB T-shirt. He stopped on the way to Kerri's place to pick up a bottle of wine. Then, as he drove past CVS, he suddenly braked and turned sharply into the parking lot. He ran in, purchased a box of condoms, then sprinted back to his car and continued on to Kerri's place.

The box of condoms stayed in the car, but a few went into one of the roomy pockets of his pants with a grin.

Tonight her usual black yoga pants tied with a loose drawstring hung low on her hips. A snug pink tank top outlined clearly braless breasts, and her nipples drew his helpless gaze. She smiled when she opened the door to him, but her eyes held a hint of reserve. Things weren't going to get weird again, were they?

He wanted to grab her, kiss her—basically jump her sexy bones—but instead he leaned forward and planted a chaste kiss on her luscious little mouth.

She'd been preparing food in the kitchen but hadn't actually started cooking yet, and he took a seat at the small counter that separated her kitchen from dining room. "Should I open the wine?"

She handed him a corkscrew and pulled two glasses out of a cupboard.

"This is nice," she approved after taking a sip. "Good choice."

"Thanks." He had no clue what it was. He'd asked the guy at the store for a nice twenty dollar bottle of white wine. He sipped his own.

"So tell me about your expansion plans," he invited. He watched her move around, turning on the stove to start water boiling for the pasta. In another pan she drizzled some olive oil. She picked up a big chef's knife and deftly flattened a couple of garlic cloves, then minced them with rapid, sure movements while she talked about her plans.

"There are so many great things about the new place." She lifted the lid to check the water. "The reception area, changing rooms, the parking…this is the time to expand. But like I said, I can't take on much more myself. I have some ideas for different types of classes, too."

He nodded, admiring her smooth graceful movements as she cooked. "That sounds great, Kerri. Your business has grown consistently since you started, so you obviously know what you're doing."

She blinked at him, seeming a little surprised, but touchingly pleased. "Thank you, Mitch. That means a lot to me."

Kerri could seem flaky at times, but she had a sharp brain and solid business training. She also had the right personality for teaching. She made it fun. Why'd she seem so surprised by the compliment?

She dumped a package of fresh pasta into the water and stirred it, then reduced the heat under it. The garlic sizzled in the pan and she added huge shrimp, a splash of the wine, some chopped tomatoes and fresh herbs.

"That smells incredible." He sniffed. "I'm starving."

She pulled a bowl of salad greens out of the fridge and tossed it with a dressing she'd already made, then popped a tray of crusty rolls into the oven to warm.

"Bread?" He raised his brows.

She laughed. "Just for you, big guy."

She drained the pasta, tossed it with the sauce and in moments they were sitting at her small dining table, feasting on perfectly al dente fettuccine, shrimp, warm bread and a tangy salad.

"Wow," Mitch said, after devouring two huge plates of pasta, a couple of rolls and a big bowl of salad. "I used to make fun of you for being a bad cook, but I think I was mistaken."

"It was just that food poisoning incident with the deli salad," she insisted with a laugh. "Really."

He grinned. "What's for dessert?"

Her face fell. "I didn't make dessert."

"Hey, I'm kidding. I'm so full, I couldn't eat a bite more. Besides, I know what I want for dessert, and it's *not* food."

He looked at her as she got his message and her eyes grew hot. "Oh."

He reached out for her hand and pulled her out of her chair and onto his lap. "I've wanted to do this ever since I got here," he growled. Spearing his fingers into her hair, he pulled her mouth to his and kissed her.

She tasted sweet and warm, her tongue teasing his, sucking gently as their mouths slid over each other, wet and open. He deepened the kiss, feeling her body soften into his as she wound her arms around his neck. "I missed you," he groaned, breaking the kiss to press his face to her exotic-smelling hair.

"I missed you too." She stroked her hands over his shoulders, then her fingers slid into his hair and grabbed hold, pulling his mouth back to her.

They kissed again, slow, sensual kisses. Mouths clinging, lifting, their breath mingling, then kissing again, deep and lingering.

Kerri broke away, gulping air into her lungs. "Whoa."

"Yeah." He paused, swallowed hard. "Want me to help with the dishes?"

"I don't feel like doing dishes right now," she confessed. "But I guess we should clean up a little."

Reluctantly he let her off his lap, his hard-on throbbing. He watched her cute little ass as she walked away from him, carrying their plates. He gathered up the rest of the dishes and helped load the dishwasher, both of them eyeing each other hungrily, the air thick around them. As she bent over to put a plate in the dishwasher, he moved up behind her and pressed his erection into her lush little behind, slid his arms around her. She straightened, put an arm up behind her to curve around his neck and he nuzzled her ear.

"You said you went out last night," he murmured, inhaling her scent. "Where'd you go?"

"Oh. Um, I went out with Liam. Remember?"

He froze. He abruptly released her and stepped back. She turned to face him and he stared at her. "You...what?"

14

"I went out with Liam. Liam Moffatt. You fixed me up with him. Remember?"

Jealousy churned in his stomach, burning and rising from his gut to his chest, which was so tight it hurt. He took a deep breath but the tightness didn't go away. He shook his head.

"Jesus Christ," he finally managed. "You went out with him?"

Her eyes were wide, wary. "Yes."

He shook his head again in disbelief. "Are you fucking crazy?"

Her face closed up. "No, I am not *fucking crazy*, thank you very much," she said, looking confused. "You're the one who introduced us, remember?"

He ignored her. "You went out with Liam," he repeated.

She stared at him. "But...wait, Mitch. Just hold on here. I don't know what you're all bent out of shape about. You're the one who introduced us."

"Yeah. But that was...before."

"Before what? Before we had sex?"

He took several deep breaths. In. Out. Control. "Yeah," he said finally, the nausea still rolling in his stomach. "Before we had sex."

"We never did talk the other night." Her fingers twirled a strand of hair around one finger. "But I know you aren't looking for any kind of long-term relationship. I know what you think of marriage." Her smile might have held a hint of regret. "So, it's okay. Don't worry. I'm not going to push for anything. We'll just go on being friends. Only now it will be friends with benefits."

"Friends with benefits," he repeated stupidly. Jesus. He thrust a hand through his hair, leaned back against her kitchen counter. "Benefits" did not begin to express what had happened between them, but whatever.

"Yes." She nodded. "You know…fuck buddies."

"Christ," he said again, temporarily robbed of vocabulary. This was not going exactly like he'd planned. "And you…you're okay with that?"

She smiled tentatively. "Well, sure. I don't really understand what happened, but I think we were both so hot and bothered we just couldn't help it. Maybe this is what we need…you know, some kind of tension release. But we can still be friends, right?"

He stared at her with incredulous stupefaction. Then he shook his head. "You know what," he said slowly. "I just cooled off."

She stared at him in dismay. "But…Mitch…"

He forced a smile. "Thanks for dinner, Kerr. I gotta go. I'll talk to you later this week." He left her staring after him with a bewildered look on her face.

In his car his eyes fell gloomily and regretfully on the box of condoms.

⚜

Kerri stood trembling in her kitchen, her hand to her mouth, her mind a scramble of confusion.

What had just happened? They'd had such a nice

dinner and things were just heating up and then…wham! They had a big fight again. Almost like he was jealous of Liam. But he had no reason to think they had an exclusive relationship. Hell, what kind of relationship *did* they have?

All she knew for sure was that they were friends. Friends who were having sex. And, since he'd stormed out in a big sulk, maybe they weren't even friends any more.

She swallowed back tears that threatened as she stared at the pots still sitting in the sink, then she mindlessly set to scrubbing, dropping stuff in the dishwasher, and wiping counters until her little kitchen was spotless. She dried her hands on a towel and looked around the kitchen which now showed no signs of the wonderful dinner they'd shared together, talking, laughing, just like it used to be — except even better with a little added zing of sexual anticipation.

As usual, yoga was her salvation, and she went into her bedroom to stretch and move through some asanas. She needed some major chakra balancing. She was going to have to read up on more than just tantra the way things were going. Her mind had never been so messed up.

She lay down on her bedroom floor and did some warm-up moves. Rising, she moved through the sun salutation several times, varying it slightly each time. Finally, she lay down for shavasana, feet apart, arms at her sides, and closed her eyes.

Of course, laying there with her eyes closed was when she started thinking about Mitch.

The phone interrupted her confused thoughts. Hailey wanted to get a bunch of people together to go to a wine tasting event being held at the Biltmore on Friday night. Kerri was happy to do anything that would take her mind off Mitch.

She couldn't stop thinking about how he'd stormed out earlier.

Maybe she just needed to give up on her friendship with Mitch.

It made her hurt inside to think that but she really didn't know what else to do.

❦

Kerri had actually gotten the idea for one of her new classes from Mitch, even though he wouldn't come to yoga. Maybe guys would come if it was an all-guys class. She could even target it to executives. Tell them it would improve their bottom line. She snorted as she worked on her computer. Bottom line was everything to business people. But still, there were definite tangible business benefits she could sell.

Also, her kids class — what a great idea. She loved kids and had five nieces and nephews under the age of ten. Sela's kids were older now, they came to her regular classes, but her two brothers' children would love it. She knew how the excess energy of the boys drove their mothers crazy sometimes. This would help them calm down, focus their energy, and she could do it in a way that would appeal to kids.

She had also added classes at different times to the schedule, now that she had additional instructors to take those on. Dianna and Kim both seemed eager and enthusiastic, reminding her of herself. So that must mean they'd be a good fit. They were off to L.A. to take an instructors' course next week and then they'd be ready to go.

When Liam called to ask if she wanted to go out Friday night, she'd already made those plans with Hailey to go to the wine tasting. Somehow, though, she found herself asking him to join them. It wasn't a date, she told herself, although even if it was, she didn't know why she felt a need to justify it.

Why shouldn't she invite him along? Why shouldn't she go out with him for that matter? She and Mitch hadn't exactly sorted out what was happening with their relationship. In fact, she hadn't heard from him all week, the jerk. Besides, Hailey knew Liam, so this was actually a chance for him to reconnect with people at home after being away for so long.

She called Hailey back and told her she was bringing Liam along.

"Oh," Hailey said.

"Is that a problem? I thought a bunch of us were going."

"No, not a problem. Not at all. I'd like to see Liam again. It's just…"

"What?"

"Well, Mitch is coming."

Kerri was silent. Her body tensed but she said, "So? He knows Liam. He introduced us, remember?"

"Oh, yeah, that's right," Hailey said brightly. "Okay, we're meeting at eight o'clock. I'm going to get tickets ahead of time so we'll all meet in the lobby."

So Mitch would be there. Fine. She shivered, remembering how angry he'd been when she'd mentioned going out with Liam. Mitch probably wouldn't be overjoyed to see him there with her. Was she pushing his buttons too far? Or was she just living her life?

⁂

Friday was not one of Mitch's better days.

He had a number of extremely adversarial divorce cases going on, and he found himself even more disgusted by some of the behavior, not just of the opposing counsel and their clients, but of his own clients.

Then he got a call that rocked his world.

It was Garth Layton. "Bob Sinclair died yesterday," he told Mitch, his voice determinedly steady. "Just thought I'd let you know. So you can tell his b—sorry, his ex-wife, there won't be any more custody issues."

Jesus Christ. Mitch covered his eyes. "Health issues?" he asked wearily.

"Yeah. He had terminal cancer. They actually gave him six months, but obviously...they were wrong." His voice was a touch bitter now.

"Shit."

"Yeah. Well. Just so you know."

"I'm sorry, Garth." He didn't know what else to say.

"Yeah. Me too."

"If I'd known...I would have tried harder...why didn't he ask to see his daughter sooner?"

Garth snorted. "She's your client. You know better than I do why."

He sighed. "Yeah. Jesus." He shook his head.

"Can't take it too personally," Garth said, although he clearly was. Mitch was too.

When he hung up, he slid down in his chair and covered his face with his hands. His chest actually hurt. He couldn't be having a heart attack, he was too young. Wasn't he?

He gave himself a few moments. Nah, it wasn't a heart attack, just stress. Christ, this work was going to kill him. He'd never thought that. He loved a good fight. He loved taking on worthy opponents, coming up with stunning, convincing arguments, getting people to do things his way...shit.

He needed a drink. No, he needed Kerri. He picked up the phone.

But his day was not destined to get better.

15

Both Liam and Mitch had offered to pick her up, but she figured it was probably better just to meet them at the hotel. So Kerri was standing in the lobby of the elegant Biltmore Hotel with Hailey waiting for the others when Mitch arrived. He greeted Hailey warmly, Kerri not so much. In fact he was downright cool.

Her heart sank. When he'd called that afternoon to talk about picking her up tonight, it was the first time she'd heard from him since he left her place Monday night, apparently pissed off about her date with Liam. She'd wanted so badly to say yes, but how could she do that when she'd already turned down Liam's offer of a ride? God, things were complicated.

The silence had vibrated with tension after she'd told Mitch she planned to meet everyone there. She didn't tell him why she was saying no. Two men had offered to take her and she didn't think she could show up with one or the other. And Mitch had sounded kind of down to start with, which made her feel even worse.

She stood there, smiling, listening to Hailey and Miguel and Mitch talk as they were joined by a few other couples. Then Liam arrived. Kerri waved to him across the lobby and he joined the group.

Painfully aware of Mitch in her peripheral vision, Kerri introduced Liam to her friends. He remembered Hailey and even knew Jason, Miguel's best man, from college.

Mitch shook his hand and greeted him too, but his tight mouth and glittering eyes made her nervous. As Hailey handed out tickets and they turned to go into the ballroom where the event was being held, he came up beside her and murmured in her ear, "Did you invite him?"

She glanced at him, a knot of fear inside her stomach. "Yes. I thought it would be a good chance for him to connect with some old friends."

He nodded tightly and followed the group into the ballroom.

She felt Mitch's eyes on her, watching her and Liam. Watching Liam stick to her side like duct tape while she tried to be polite and friendly but not encourage him. While she tried to ignore the fact that she really only wanted to be with Mitch.

She tried to get into the wine tasting, learning about various types of grapes and how white wines actually ranged in color from green to yellow to brown, and red wines weren't just red but ranged from a pale red to a deep brown red, becoming lighter in color as they aged. She learned that whereas time improves many red wines, it ruins most white wines. She carefully tried to follow the three steps of wine tasting, the first impression, the taste and the aftertaste, trying to judge the body and texture of the wines she tasted. Several wineries from the Santa Barbara area participated in the fundraiser for a new homeless shelter.

When Liam slid an arm around her waist as they moved from one tasting station to another, she felt Mitch's gaze burning into her. After a while, she wasn't the only one who noticed. Hailey kept casting worried looks between the two of them, and Liam asked quietly, "Is he pissed off at me about something? If looks could kill, I'd be lying on the floor back there bleeding."

She laughed shortly. "He's always pissed off about something, lately. Don't worry about it."

"You two *are* just friends aren't you?" Liam sent an uneasy glance at Mitch.

"Apparently not any more." Her throat ached as she sipped her wine.

She smiled more warmly at Liam than she intended and he smiled back at her and took her hand. Carefully, she removed her fingers from his grasp as they moved on.

Liam thought she wanted to be with him. She only wanted to be with Mitch. And who knew what Mitch wanted, the way he kept scowling and muttering. Thank God she had brought her own car, which she so rarely drove, and could make her exit as quickly as possible.

Mitch tried to resist, but after watching Kerri with Liam all night, he couldn't get the idea out of his head. He watched her leave, alone, and he drove to her home, drawn inexorably.

All week long he'd been wrestling with this "fuck buddies" thing. Christ, could she really be serious? She intended for them to go on being friends, just sleeping together for a little extra fun. And was she planning to keep seeing other guys, too? Apparently so, since she'd invited Liam tonight.

Throughout the week he'd gotten more and more pissed off about being "friends with benefits", and the news today about Bob Sinclair's death had just added to his irritation. And to top it all off, Liam had showed up.

He hadn't been this pent up and pissed off for God knew how long.

He searched the darkness for any signs of Liam. Since no other cars were parked outside her condo, he climbed out of his SUV and walked up to Kerri's door. After he rang the bell, he leaned his forehead on the door, waiting, heart thudding painfully in his chest.

She opened the door, eyebrows raised, lips parted. "Mitch! What are you doing here?"

He pushed inside, not hard, just determinedly, and closed the door carefully behind him. "We're fuck buddies, right?" He set his hands on her shoulders. "What do you think I'm here for?"

16

He watched Kerri's eyes widen, and darken. Her lips parted. He bent his head, taking her mouth in a demanding, urgent kiss, anger and frustration surging inside him. He thrust his tongue inside her warm, velvety mouth and kissed her with all the built-up frustration he'd felt all week, taking her mouth again and again.

She responded, though, after a moment of surprise. Her body softened and leaned into him and then she was kissing him back just as furiously as he was, their mouths feverish, grinding against one another in a fierce attempt to apparently devour each other.

Desire mounted in him, hardened him, ignited him. It was unstoppable, and she met him equally, both of them panting and moaning, wrapping themselves around each other.

When he finally left in the early hours of the morning, they were sated and exhausted.

And Mitch hated himself for what he'd done.

He'd never even told Kerri why he'd been in such a miserable mood to start with. And the main reason he'd wanted to see her was to talk to her, not to fuck her. She was a good listener. Her contemplative nature, always trying to understand the deeper questions in life, often provided good insight and reassurance to him. Even though he was so cynical after all the crap he'd seen at work, she had an optimism and powerful compassion that encouraged him and kept him going.

Instead, all he'd done was use her for sex.

Shame burned him and his gut churned with regret and remorse. Damn, he shouldn't have done that.

He tried to justify it in his mind. That's what she wanted, right? That's what she'd said. She wasn't looking for anything more, she expected their relationship to be friends with benefits.

Well, the benefits part was great, but they were still supposed to be friends. He hadn't even talked to her, told her why he was so pissed off, apart from the fact she'd invited Liam, which he could *not* talk to her about. Not if they were supposed to go on the way they had.

He swore as he pulled into his dark driveway. Friends didn't treat friends that way. How could he live with himself? Not only was he questioning his whole career, he was now guilty of abusing his best friend. He was such an asshole.

❦

"I owe you an apology."

Mitch stood on her front door step Saturday afternoon. He looked adorably miserable, hair mussed, eyes shadowed.

She stood back and let him in, wiping her hands on a towel. What was he doing there?

"What are you doing?" he asked, sniffing.

She led the way into her kitchen, which looked like a chemistry lab with vials, jars, beakers and bottles spread everywhere. He looked around in amazement.

"Concocting." She stirred a huge pot of mysterious liquid. He frowned. "I am *not* eating that."

She laughed, and it was such a relief to have a genuine moment of amusement. "It's not for eating. It's aromatherapy oil."

"Ah." He sniffed again and peered into the vat. "You look like a mad scientist."

Suddenly conscious that she was wearing a T-shirt with oily stains and old shorts, her hair scraped back with an ugly headband, she grimaced. "Thanks."

"Seriously, is that what you're making? How do you do that?"

She started telling him about the essential oils and herbs she was using.

"What do you do with this stuff?"

She shrugged. "I use it when I get out of the shower. I give some to friends. Lately, one of the massage therapists at the spa has been using it on some of her clients. Apparently they love it."

"Oh. That's why you were asking Jack about it that night."

She nodded. "But please don't say anything to Sela. Amanda hasn't told her, and she's afraid Sela would freak out if she started using something she didn't know about."

"Secret's safe with me," he said, with a shrug.

"I'm trying some new things." There was silence other than the blurp-blurp-blurp of thick liquid as she poured it into the bottles arranged on the counter.

"Let me help. That looks heavy."

She let him take the pot and she steadied the bottles as he filled them, one after the other.

"So, um…why are you here again?" she asked, when the pot was empty. He set it down carefully.

"Oh, yeah." He picked up a towel and wiped his hands slowly, looking a little embarrassed. "I wanted to apologize. For last night."

She watched him swallow.

"You were pretty intense last night." That was an understatement. He'd shown up at her door all moody and dark, then proceeded to fuck her brains out. Not that she'd minded, but she'd definitely had the feeling something was bothering him. When he'd left in the middle of the night, although he'd kissed her good-bye, she'd still felt something wasn't right.

He nodded. "Yeah. I had a kind of shitty week."

"How come?" She looked at him steadily. "Work stuff?" Or "us stuff"? But she kept that question to herself.

"Yeah." He said it almost with relief. "Hell, yeah."

"Want to talk about it?"

He nodded and sat down on a stool at her counter. The words came pouring out, and he told her about Bob Sinclair and the frustration he'd felt about that. Kerri watched him sadly, knowing how that must have affected him, still listening as he went on to talk more about other cases and all the aggravation he'd been experiencing lately with delays in the court system, ridiculous, selfish clients and greedy counsel.

Something expanded inside Kerri, warm and soft. Mitch was her best friend and she'd never known this stuff had been bothering him so much. It said so much about him.

She capped bottles and cleaned up as she listened to him talk, and talk some more, occasionally interjecting questions.

"So what is this collaborative law you mentioned?" She set the big pot in her sink.

"It's a new alternative to dispute resolution in California. It's a third resource, after litigation and mediation. Like mediation, it uses non-adversarial techniques." He paused. "After this one case a while back, I felt like shit. I was just doing what the client wanted but afterward I knew I couldn't keep doing that kind of thing forever. So I started trying some mediation. I was hoping it might motivate me, give me the satisfaction I wasn't getting from those long court battles."

"And collaborative law?"

"It's something new I'm trying." He shrugged. "It's great, but the lawyer on the other side has to be on board with that. With collaborative law, each spouse hires their own collaborative lawyer, and we conduct settlement negotiations with them in four-way meetings. The lawyers act as advisors to the clients instead of taking charge of the process. If they can't reach agreement, the lawyers have to both withdraw, and neither of them or any other members of their firms can represent the couple in divorce litigation."

"You're kidding," she said slowly, closing up packages of fragrant but strange-looking herbs. "So if you don't agree, you don't get the case, and neither does anybody else in your firm."

He nodded. "It means all four participants have to be committed to reaching a reasonable settlement."

"But that sounds risky. Isn't litigation where the big bucks are? How did you get your firm to agree to that?"

"I have a decent track record. I suggested we try it and see how it goes. I have a pretty good idea which ones we can settle and which ones we can't."

She gazed at him for a long moment, then looked away. "You shouldn't do work that is making you unhappy. It's as simple as that, Mitch. You should do what makes you happy."

He tipped his head to one side. "Huh. Yeah. I guess."

"So this collaborative law...why don't you pursue that more? It sounds like something that would be better for you...and for everybody." She hesitated. "Is the money an issue? I would think it would be for your firm."

He considered that. "Not for me. Money's nice but it's just money. But yeah, for the firm, money can be an issue."

He shrugged. "Like I said, they trust my judgment and they're willing to take a chance on me."

"Then what's the problem? If it's going to be less stressful and give you more satisfaction, that's what you should do."

"Yeah. You're right." He looked at her and there was something warm and appreciative in his dark eyes. "Thanks, Kerri."

She leaned across the counter to plant a kiss on his surprised mouth. "I take back every lawyer joke I've ever said." Dammit, her voice choked up.

He kissed her back, hard.

"You know, you should have told me about this sooner. Keeping stuff bottled up inside you isn't healthy. It knocks your chakras out of alignment."

He laughed. "You've been a little preoccupied lately."

"I'm sorry, Mitch." She nibbled her bottom lip. "You should know better than anyone, if I start acting a little princessy just give me a smack back to reality."

"Sweetheart, your reality is just a little different than everyone else's." His smile held so much affection she didn't take offence. "I've wanted to talk to you about it. Actually last night, I really wanted to talk to you about it. I guess that's why I was so pissed about Liam being there."

She nodded. "I kind of had the feeling you weren't too happy about that." She waited, but he said nothing more.

"Wanna order some pizza?" he asked.

"Sure."

He picked up the phone and ordered pizza while she finished cleaning up her laboratory-slash-kitchen.

As they ate, they talked about their friends' upcoming wedding. "Miguel and Hailey have booked rooms for the wedding party so we can stay at the hotel that night."

Kerri nodded and caught a piece of drippy, stringy cheese. "I know. Isn't that great?"

"Want to stay with me?" he asked casually. "We can share a room."

She met his gaze steadily and her stomach did a little flip. "Sure." Ooh. Hotel sex. There was something about being in a room of their own that was almost like living together. Intimate.

Now she was looking forward to the wedding.

17

The Thursday before the wedding, Kerri passed on several bottles of her new body oil to Amanda while Sela was out for lunch. "Here." She handed Amanda the plain plastic bag, again feeling like she was making a drug deal. "There are two different kinds. The ginger is for sore muscles. The lavender one is a relaxation blend for stress relief. They're both very hydrating. The lavender one also nourishes and increases elasticity in the skin."

"Awesome!" Amanda said. "I can't wait to try them!"

Kerri returned to her office. Her new classes were filling up and for the first time ever, she had waiting lists. Even her new executive class, targeted to businessmen, was attracting some interest. Thank God both of her new instructors were working out and seemed popular with her clients. She sighed with satisfaction. Take that, Sela. Well, that was petty, but… She grinned.

That night Melanie, Hailey's matron of honor, was holding a bachelorette party. Tomorrow night was the rehearsal and rehearsal dinner, Saturday would be fully occupied with spa treatments for the wedding party at White Lotus and, of course, the long-awaited wedding.

"What exactly does she have planned for the

bachelorette party?" Sela asked Kerri curiously as she was on her way out.

"I have no idea. I hope she has some naked guys coming to dance for us."

"You do not." Sela laughed. "That would just be embarrassing."

"Yeah, you're right." Kerri grinned.

Melanie and her investment-banker husband lived in a gorgeous home in Hope Ranch. She had warned everyone not to drive so there would be no DUI infractions after the party, so Kerri took a taxi.

"Everyone's dying to know what you have planned," she said with a smile when she arrived.

"It's not going to be that naughty." Melanie laughed. "We'll play a couple of games, open presents, eat, drink, and I got a movie for us to watch."

"A movie?" Kerri raised her brows and Melanie smirked.

The others arrived and they all moved into Melanie's great room, depositing gifts on a decorated table. Melanie invited them to serve themselves punch from the bowl on a table laden with nachos, chips, pretzels and more. As Kerri dipped the ladle into the bowl, she noticed the ice floating there was in the shape of a huge penis.

Kerri collapsed against Hailey with laughter. Then Hailey pointed out the decoration: a huge cucumber with a condom on it, two plums nestled at the top and tied with curly ribbons. There were also pink paper garlands of penises strung across the room.

"Oh, Lord." Hailey set her palms to her cheeks. "What have I gotten into here?"

"We're also having Screaming Orgasms." Melanie grinned and held up a glass full of a creamy liquid.

Once everyone had arrived, Melanie sat them down to play a game. "Okay, this game is 'How well do you know your fiancé'," she began. "Hailey, what is Miguel's favorite band?"

Jackson Bang. That was Mitch's favorite band.

"Oooh." Hailey pondered that. "Right now, I would say it's Liquid."

"Right! Okay, this one is easy. Who was his best friend growing up?"

"Jason," she replied immediately.

Danny Davidson. Kerri smiled. Mitch had told her about his nerdy best friend. They'd gone their separate ways when they started college and Danny lived in New York now, but they still kept in touch.

"What sports or activities did he enjoy growing up?" Melanie continued.

"How do *you* know this stuff?" Hailey demanded.

"I e-mailed the questions to Miguel earlier this week and he sent me the answers," Melanie answered smugly.

"Oh. Okay, well I know he played a lot of basketball..."

"And..."

"Um...football?"

"Nope. Soccer."

"Oh, yes, yes, I should have known that." Hailey thumped a fist into the couch cushion with a laugh.

Kerri continued to answer the questions in her head as if they were about Mitch, pretty sure she was getting them all right. Then Melanie asked, "What's his favorite sexual position?"

Everyone screamed with laughter and Hailey turned pink. "I can't answer that!"

"Oh, come on!"

She sighed and grinned. "Okay, he likes it when I'm on top." Then she frowned. "Did you really ask him that?"

Melanie laughed. "Oh, yeah. And you're right!"

"Oooh, Hailey," the girls teased.

Kerri laughed too, but she didn't know what Mitch's favorite position was—they hadn't even tried very many. He seemed to like her on top, her underneath... She became very warm and tried to focus her attention back on the party.

The gifts, in keeping with the theme of the evening, ranged from gorgeous silk lingerie, to a naughty black merry widow, to some flavored massage oils and chocolate body paint.

"You guys are going to have so much fun on your honeymoon," Melanie said as everyone oohed and aahed over the gifts, throwing in the odd crude joke as well.

Finally Melanie started the movie she'd chosen.

"I'm not sure I'm up for any hard core porn," Hailey warned as they all got comfortable.

"Not to worry," Melanie assured her. "I specifically looked for something for women. They actually have a whole section of women's porn on this website I found."

"Oh, God, Mel."

"This movie is apparently like those romance novels you like to read, Hailey."

"Oh, no!" Laurel, the third bridesmaid, cried. "I want to see some skin!"

"Oh, there'll be skin, all right."

The movie started and to everyone's relief, including Kerri, it wasn't hard core. It actually had a story, and yes, it was a romance, and the sex, while explicit, was totally part of the story. In fact, it was hot, hot, *hot*, including a little threesome that was disturbingly sexy.

Kerri grew warm and wet watching the movie, squeezeing her thighs together discreetly. As the movie continued, she got more and more turned on. She was going to have to go see Mitch tonight. He probably wouldn't mind. By the time the movie ended, it was clear all the other girls were feeling equally as aroused.

"No fair," Laurel complained. "Melanie's husband is upstairs. I'm betting he gets lucky tonight. Hailey has Miguel to go home to. Everyone has someone except me and Kerri. We're going to be all lonely and frustrated tonight."

Without thinking, Kerri blurted out, "Not me."

Heads all whipped around to look at her with raised eyebrows.

She smiled weakly.

18

"Kerri!?" Hailey and Melanie said together. "You have some guy stashed at home?"

"Is it Liam?"

She shook her head. "No." She regretted opening her mouth. "Never mind."

Well, there was no way any of them were taking that, they were all over her to tell what she'd meant, and finally she confessed what had happened between her and Mitch.

"I knew it!" Hailey said. "You two were meant to be together."

"Don't get all excited," Kerri warned. "All we're doing is having sex. We're fuck buddies."

At the look of stunned incredulity on all their faces, she laughed. "What?"

There was another moment of silence, then Hailey smiled tightly. "Well, I'm speechless."

"How long has this been going on?" Laurel demanded.

"Not long," Kerri said, a little dreamily, remembering their first kiss. "One day we were having a big fight and wham, he kissed me."

"Oh, God." Hailey moaned.

"Things were kind of weird after that, but then, the night of the grand opening party we just couldn't keep our hands off each other. We went back to my place and…did it."

Everyone sighed.

"That was the night you two were so pissy with each other," Hailey said with dawning understanding. "But Kerri, that's not like you. Casual sex is *so* not you."

"I know." Kerri sighed. "But it's soooo good."

"Oh, God," Laurel said. "Please, take me with you. You can share him. We could have a little threesome, like in the movie."

Kerri was so turned on from watching the movie and talking about Mitch, not to mention a tiny bit tipsy from the punch and a couple of Screaming Orgasms, that for a wild moment she actually considered that idea. Laurel was attractive, Mitch always joked about his biggest fantasy being girl on girl action, maybe…

No. She regained her senses. Talk about risking a friendship. She and Laurel would never be able to look each other in the eye again, never mind her and Mitch.

She forced a laugh. "I'm not sharing."

Amid laughter and teasing, a taxi was called that could take some of them home and Kerri felt very naughty and daring when she gave the driver Mitch's address.

***

The doorbell ringing over and over woke Mitch from his sound sleep. He staggered out of bed and headed to the door before he groggily realized he was naked. He grabbed a pair of plaid boxers from a chair and stumbled clumsily into them, the insistent ring of the bell digging into his brain.

He threw open the door. Kerri stood there, leaning against the wall, smiling a sultry smile, wearing snug, low-slung jeans and a black ribbed tank top with a glittery design on the front.

He rubbed his eyes. Maybe he was dreaming.

"Can I come in?" she asked, voice husky.

He could not get a word out, just gawked at her. Giving his head a shake, he stood aside so she could enter. "What...are you doing here?" he managed to say thickly, rubbing his chest.

Kerri's eyes darkened as she studied him. She pushed the door closed behind her and turned back to him, running her hands over his chest. He swallowed hard.

"I needed to see you," she purred.

"I thought you were out with the girls..."

"I was." She rubbed his pecs, his hard nipples, and got a choked gasp from him. "We watched a dirty movie and I got so turned on I had to come see you."

His eyes widened, but his hands went automatically to her narrow waist. She pressed herself against him, fisted her hands in his hair and held his head as she kissed him. God.

Her mouth was sweet, fruity and warm, and her little tongue pushed into his mouth determinedly, stroking his. She immediately had his attention as his body hardened in response. He was wide awake and ready to go. She rubbed up against him urgently, obviously feeling his hard-on through the thin cotton of the boxers, and nipped at his bottom lip.

"We had Screaming Orgasms," she told him in a husky voice.

He tried to clear his head. Holy shit. What had they been doing?

"It's a drink." She pushed on his chest, still nibbling on his mouth and chin, moving him backward down the hall toward his bedroom. "Now I want a real one."

After, they lay in Mitch's bed, drowsy and boneless,

Kerri sprawled across his chest, stroking him. His hand moved over her back as he lay staring into the dark.

"Do you mind that I came here?" she asked sleepily.

He looked up at the ceiling. He felt kind of strange, considering he'd just had a mind-blowing orgasm and held her in his arms while she came. Talk about a screaming orgasm. "Um, no. That was awesome."

"Good." Her fingers slid up over his shoulder. "Laurel wanted to come, too."

"What!" he choked out. He felt her smile against his chest.

"We were all turned on from watching that movie. Everyone else had husbands or fiancés to go home to, except her and me. Then I made the mistake of telling everyone I was going to come see you." She lifted her head and peered at him in the darkness. "Is...is that a problem?"

He moved his head, a bit confused. "You told them we're...sleeping together?"

She nodded, biting her bottom lip. "Yeah. I didn't want people to know, but it kind of slipped out."

He looked at her and discovered he could care less if people knew about them. In fact, he was glad. Somehow it made it seem less sleazy. "It's okay," he managed to say, his hands relaxing on her bare skin again.

"So anyway," she continued with some relief, laying her head back down. "Laurel wanted me to share you. Like the threesome in the movie."

"Jesus," he said in a strangled voice.

"And I was almost tempted," she continued, causing his heart to stop beating. "Because I know you have that fantasy..."

"You have got to be kidding."

"Yeah. Isn't that your ultimate fantasy?" Her fingers curved over his shoulder, her thumb stroking his clavicle.

"Not any more."

"Oh. Then what is your ultimate fantasy?"

"Um…Kerri…"

"You can tell me," she coaxed.

There was a long pause. Finally he said, "Naked yoga."

"Hmm?" She lifted her head again. "Naked yoga? Explain."

"You're teaching a yoga class and you're naked. I'm in the class and I'm naked. Everybody's naked. You're demonstrating poses and I can see everything, and then you're helping me and you're putting your hands all over my body."

"The whole class is naked?"

"Yeah…although they don't figure very prominently in the scenario. Guess I have a bit of exhibitionist in me."

"A bit!" She laughed. "Remember that pool party where you guys were having a contest jumping off the diving board to see who could get their shorts off before you hit the water?"

He chuckled. "Were you watching that?"

"Me and about twenty other people. So, hmm, naked yoga. Sounds…intriguing."

"Don't even think of adding *that* class to your schedule."

"I don't know…there might be good money in that…" Her voice faded into drowsiness. He smiled and they drifted off to sleep in each other's arms.

⟳⟲

Mitch's alarm woke them at seven-thirty. Kerri started to struggle out of a deep sleep while Mitch climbed out of bed, turned back to her and gently pushed her hair off her face to kiss her. "Stay here if you want," he whispered against her mouth. "I know you don't have to go to work as early as I do."

She drifted back to sleep for a while, then got up and had just finished dressing when Karma chimed on her cell phone in her purse.

It was Hailey. "Where are you?"

"Mitch's place."

"Still?"

"Mmm. I was just going home to shower and change. Mitch left for work a while ago." She wandered over to the dresser in his room and ran her eyes over the assortment of personal items…some change, sticky notes with cryptic scribbles from work, a dry cleaning tag.

"I want to take you for lunch."

"Aren't you kind of busy? You're getting married tomorrow."

She drifted into Mitch's living room to find her shoes. She'd always liked Mitch's house. Maybe that was because she'd helped him pick it out. They'd gone around looking at houses together, and it had been a big joke when the realtor thought they were married. Mitch had wanted her opinion before he made the offer on this one and she totally agreed this Craftsman bungalow was the one for him.

"I have time for lunch. I need to talk to you."

"Okay, I'll meet you at Darby's."

"Excellent."

⟨⟨⟩⟩

They sat on the small wooden deck shaded by a big fig tree outside Darby's, and Hailey ordered a bacon, lettuce, tomato and avocado sandwich. Kerri ordered a salad.

They made conversation until their meals arrived and Kerri asked, "So what did you want to talk to me about?"

Hailey pressed her lips together. "I want to talk about you and Mitch."

Kerri raised a brow as she pushed her fork into a piece of avocado.

"This friends with benefits thing," Hailey continued.

"What about it?"

Hailey looked down at her sandwich. "It's such a bad idea."

Kerri stared at her. "Why do you say that?"

"Look, I'm a high school teacher. I see kids doing this all the time. It's an easy way for them to not have to deal with serious relationship issues at their age. But it always ends up bad, and it's almost always bad for the girl."

Kerri tipped her head to one side. "We're not teenagers, Hailey."

"I know, but the problems are the same. In this friends with benefits thing, the guys are the only ones who get the 'benefits'." She made air quotes with her fingers.

Kerri grinned. "I wouldn't say that. The benefits are pretty good for me."

A smile tugged at Hailey's lips, but she went on. "Right now, maybe. But women aren't made like that. *You're* not made like that. You go on having sex with Mitch, and your emotions are going to get involved whether you want it or not. It just happens. Then you want more than just friends with benefits and he doesn't. And someone ends up getting hurt."

Kerri wanted to squirm in her seat listening to Hailey.

"You're both my friends." Hailey leaned forward. "I don't want either of you to get hurt. And if *you're* just using Mitch for sex, maybe *he's* the one who's going to get hurt."

Kerri pursed her lips. "I'm not using him for sex."

"Really? Then what was last night?"

Kerri didn't want to answer that. She *had* used Mitch for sex. But it wasn't like he didn't get anything out of it. He'd been only too willing. She set down her fork and gazed at her plate. Her throat tightened and she swallowed painfully.

She pushed her half-eaten salad away.

"The kids at school talk to me, I guess because I'm not that much older than they are," Hailey said. "Especially the girls. I've heard this Jack and Jill story so many times."

"Jack and Jill?"

Hailey waved a hand. "That's what they call it."

Kerri sighed.

"Will you think about it?" Hailey asked.

Kerri looked at her. "It's kind of late for that. We've already crossed that line. How do I go back?"

19

ailey's words ran through Kerri's mind for the rest of the day, including the wedding rehearsal and the dinner afterward at Hailey's parents' home.

As she talked and laughed with friends and Hailey and Miguel's families, she was constantly aware of Mitch nearby, the way he looked at her, his eyes warm, his smile affectionate. It made her feel good that they were friends again, but damned if his just *looking* at her didn't turn her on, too. How was she supposed to go back to being just friends if she got wet every time he smiled at her?

She smiled back at him across the poolside patio where he stood talking to some of the guys.

Liam had called her Thursday afternoon to invite her out, and she'd regretfully told him she couldn't see him again. The first "normal" guy she'd gone out with in a while, and she just was flat out not interested in him.

Maybe she was making a mistake in turning him down, after Hailey's dire predictions. If things between her and Mitch were really just friends with benefits, there was no reason she couldn't keep pursuing her goal of finding a husband. And she really, really needed a husband.

The only problem was, she no longer had any interest in any other guys.

Oh, man, Hailey was so right. She was in big trouble.

◯◯◌

The White Lotus spa had been booked for the entire afternoon by the wedding party so they could get ready for the wedding there. The girls and Hailey's mother had manicures and pedicures, salt rubs and hot stone massages to exfoliate and relax them, and after, they all had their hair and makeup done.

Kerri didn't usually wear much makeup and when she did, she thought she did a pretty good job, so someone else doing it gave her visions of clownish red cheeks and lips.

"I know, I know," Danica soothed. "You want a natural look." Kerri submitted to her brushes and tools and when Danica turned her to the mirror, her skin glowed subtly, eyes shadowed and enhanced, and her lips gleamed a nice berry color, not too bright.

"Hey. It looks nice."

Danica grinned. "Finishing touch." She whipped the cape off Kerri's shoulders and dusted her shoulders and chest with the same golden shimmer she'd used on her face.

"Who's my next victim?"

When Danica was finished, they all admired each other, but Hailey especially glowed.

"I'm giving you each one of these lipsticks," Danica said. "You'll have to touch up the glossy topcoat, but the color should last all day. Maybe after dinner touch up your color too. Laurel, yours is a different color, you can't wear that berry color with that red hair." She handed them each a double-ended tube which Kerri examined doubtfully. Lipstick that lasted all day?

"And the good thing about this stuff is, you can even kiss and it doesn't come off on the other person."

Kerri kissed the back of her hand and held it up to show the others, amazed.

"Now for the hair."

Again, doubts fluttered inside Kerri. "It's not long enough to put up," she told Angel, the hair stylist.

"Sure it is. Just wait." Angel started curling Kerri's wavy hair and Kerri closed her eyes apprehensively. But when it was done, Angel had swept her hair loosely back in waves, her long bangs and a few tendrils framing her face. "Oh. That's nice." She turned her head to one side, then the other.

"I've got to get started on Hailey," Angel said. "It's going to take a while."

The bridesmaids gathered in a different room to dress. The girls all wore identical cobalt blue, bias-cut slip dresses, cut low in the back, with tiny straps, which flattered all of them.

"We look gooooood!" Laurel cried and they all laughed.

Hailey emerged from the other room moments later and they all gasped.

"Hailey, you look so beautiful I'm going to cry," Kerri said, her throat tight. She blinked rapidly and smiled. Hailey's dress was a similar style to theirs, ivory bias-cut silk with pearls and crystals on the bodice and straps. Instead of a veil, pearls and crystals sparkled in an intricate arrangement in her hair.

Kerri produced a bottle of champagne and poured them all a glass. "I'd like to make a toast to Hailey, with thanks for not making us wear hideous poofy bridesmaid dresses!"

"To Hailey!"

The photographer waited for them to do some photos before they left for the church. The spa provided some excellent photo locations, in front of the French doors leading to the yoga studio, in front of the huge arched window at the front, and in the lounge.

Then it was time to leave for the church in the limo. Kerri tossed her overnight bag in with all the things she'd need for the next day. A thrill ran through her at the thought of spending the night with Mitch. Hotel sex.

Miguel and his attendants waited at the front of the beautiful church. As musicians played Pachelbel on violin and piano, Laurel started down the aisle, followed by Kerri then Melanie. When Kerri arrived at the front, Mitch caught her eye and winked, and she smiled back at him. God, he looked gorgeous in that black tux.

They all turned to watch Hailey walk down the aisle on her father's arm to begin the very traditional ceremony. Afterward, as they left the church, Mitch paired up with Kerri, holding out his arm for her to take as they walked back up the aisle.

"You are the sexiest bridesmaid I've ever seen," he murmured in her ear, and she shivered and ducked her head briefly.

The bridal party drank champagne in the limo on the way to the resort where the reception was being held. In contrast to the traditional ceremony, the reception was much more relaxed. After a gourmet meal, the party really got started with dancing under the stars in the open air gazebo. White lights twinkled in the palm trees and in the masses of white tulle hanging on the walls and around the tables. A soft breeze off the nearby Pacific Ocean flickered the flames of the candles glowing on every table.

⌒◈⌒

"I think we have to dance together now," Kerri said to Mitch.

Mitch turned to look at her. Oh, yeah. She was one

smokin' hot bridesmaid. He took her hand and they joined the rest of the wedding party on the dance floor. They'd danced together many, many times—fast, slow, they'd even learned to swing dance together. But tonight, the feel of Kerri's small, firm body so close to him gave him strange feelings—a possessive urge to hold her close, to not let anyone else near her, to drag her up to their room and screw her senseless.

He held her closer than he usually did, wanting to feel her body against his. He'd been watching her tits jiggle lusciously under the silk dress all day, tormenting him, and he wanted to feel them against him.

But he wanted more.

When she'd come to his place the other night, of course he'd taken what she'd offered. And he'd given in return. But afterward he'd felt…used. He couldn't help but be amused at the irony of it. He was being used for sex. Every guy's wet dream. What could be better?

He wanted more. He needed to tell Kerri—but how?

"What are you thinking?" she asked softly. "You look worried."

He hesitated, then said, "I'm worried about whether I'll represent Hailey or Miguel when the divorce happens."

Kerri stared at him open-mouthed.

"I've known Hailey longer," he continued blandly. "But Miguel is a good buddy now."

"I can't believe you just said that," she said slowly, drawing away from him. "At their wedding!"

He shrugged. "Marriage is crazy."

Shit, that wasn't what he'd meant to say at all. He swallowed a groan at his own cowardly stupidity.

"Do you really believe they'll end up divorced?"

"Nah." He turned her expertly with a little pressure of his right hand. "They'll make it."

She looked at him as if she didn't believe him. The song ended and they moved apart. Kerri walked away from him and there was no mistaking the coolness in her demeanor.

Mitch noticed Hailey giving them the eye and she didn't look happy. What was up with that?

He ran a hand through his hair and went back to his seat at the head table to find his half-finished beer. The more he tried to hide his true feelings, the worse he made things.

While he sat there staring moodily at the dancing crowd, Laurel appeared and slid into the chair beside him.

"Hey." He forced a smile.

"Hey yourself." She smiled back flirtatiously.

Warning bells went off in his head. Uncomfortably, he remembered Kerri's liquored-up confession that Laurel had wanted to join them in a threesome. His dick stirred at the idea, but his mind closed off that train of thought.

"Having fun?"

"Sure." He shifted slightly away from her as she leaned closer. "How about you?"

"Oh, yeah." She moved closer again. "Listen, Kerri told me that you and she are...well, having sex. But you're just sex pals. So, if you're looking for another sex pal..."

Incredulous, Mitch stared at her and she laid her hand on his shoulder, her thumb stroking his neck. He put a hand up to cover hers, intending to remove it from his shoulder, and his gaze fell on Kerri across the room, watching them with wide eyes and an open mouth. Then she whirled around and darted out of the room into the dark gardens outside the gazebo.

Mitch's heart stopped momentarily, then thudded painfully. He removed Laurel's hand gently from his shoulder and placed it on the table, and stood. He laughed, trying to save face for Laurel. She'd probably had too much too drink and would be embarrassed about this tomorrow. "Yeah right." He forced a smile. "You can do way better than me, Laurel." He shook his head ruefully, flashed another smile and strode away, following Kerri.

Glowing lights lit the way along the brick path through the shrubs and palm trees of the resort. He followed the path, not sure which way Kerri had gone, until the music faded behind him, accompanied by the soft chirrups of crickets in the dark shrubbery. The path curved around a palm tree and he spotted her ahead. She had left the path and was leaning against the smooth trunk of a palm, her head resting against it, her back to him. He stopped momentarily, unsure how he was going to approach this. He'd wanted to apologize for what he'd said earlier, but seeing the look on her face when she'd seen him with Laurel made him wonder...hope...

"Kerri," he called softly.

She whirled around. "Oh. You startled me." Her face was indistinct in the darkness but he saw her quickly raise a hand to her cheek and swipe. Ah shit. She was crying.

"Sorry." He moved closer and she turned away from him again. He cupped her bare shoulders, her skin silky and cool in the night air. She tensed beneath his hands. "I'm sorry, Kerri."

"Sorry for what?" She leaned her forehead against the smooth trunk of the tree.

"For being so cynical about Hailey and Miguel."

"Oh."

"When you asked what I was worried about, that wasn't really it."

"Then why did you say that?"

He paused, enjoying the feel of her slim shoulders under his hands, her skin flower petal soft. "Because I didn't want to tell you what I was really thinking about."

There was a beat of silence. "What were you really thinking about?"

"I was thinking about you."

Still she said nothing. She was letting him do all the work here. Perspiration dampened his forehead and stung his armpits.

"Liam called me on Thursday."

Mitch gave his head a little shake at the conversational leap.

"He asked me out again."

It was like a fist in the gut. "Oh." His hands tightened on her.

"Is that a problem?"

He couldn't hide his anger. "Shit."

"You're the one who fixed me up with him. Remember?"

"Oh, yeah, I remember," he said curtly. "Stupid idiot that I was. I should never have agreed to that. Are you going to go?"

"No."

Again a pause. The music and crickets faded away, the only sound Mitch could hear was his heart beating heavily.

"Why not?"

"I don't want to see him again."

Say it, damn it. Say it.

"Why did you run away when you saw Laurel talking to me?" he asked instead.

Silence. Her head tipped down. "Don't," she whispered.

Her shoulders vibrated beneath his hands and he slid them down her smooth arms. He was putting it out there, but not in so many words. Was she brave enough to meet him?

"Tell me," he murmured, bending his head to press his mouth to the soft curve where her neck met her shoulder. He inhaled her scent and it made him dizzy.

"Mitch, why did you sleep with me?"

Oh Christ. He dragged in a breath. "I slept with you because I...because you're...okay, screw it." He was going to do it.

20

*M*itch felt like he was about to jump out of an airplane, hoping like hell his parachute worked, hurtling into a gut-wrenching free fall, not knowing where it would end.

"Ever since you came up with this crazy idea that you wanted to find a husband, I've been going nuts. I can't stand the thought of you with another guy. I want you for myself. Okay?"

"Like…a girlfriend?" she whispered hesitantly.

"Yeah." He blew out a long breath. "Like a girlfriend. I was jealous of Liam, because after we slept together I thought that meant we were moving into a different kind of relationship. You know."

"Oh." Her body softened against his. "Mitch. Why didn't you say that?"

"Christ, I didn't know I *had* to say it," he said, just a little defensively. "I thought I *showed* you how I felt. I thought you would *know* after we slept together, that's what that meant. And then, you were all, 'we'll be fuck buddies', like the fact that we just had the most unbelievable sex of my life meant nothing."

"Oh." She breathed out a long sigh at that. "I thought that's what you wanted. You don't want a commitment. You don't do long term relationships."

"What did you want?" Mitch asked. He pressed another kiss to the side of her neck and her throat moved as she swallowed.

"I just wanted you."

His heart grew warm in his chest, spreading heat throughout his body.

"So why did you run out here just now?" he murmured. "Tell me, Kerri."

"I saw you with Laurel and...God, I can't believe it...I was jealous."

Thank Christ. He let out a breath he didn't realize he'd been holding. "Nothing was happening," he told her, truthfully from his point of view. "I only want you, Kerri." He pressed himself against her, nudging his hard-on into her ass. His hands slid from her arms to her waist then around in front of her and she gave a little moan. He pulled her back against him, away from the tree, and turned her in his arms so he could look her in the eyes.

"I don't know what will happen with us," he said softly. "I can't predict the future. If things don't work out between us, yeah, there's a chance you'll hate my guts. To me, losing you as a friend is a pretty big risk. Do you think I'd take that big a risk for a few nights of sex?" He shook his head. "I was having freakin' nightmares about you with those other guys. What you were doing." He buried his face in her hair. "Kerri, I don't want you to see other guys. Just me."

She made a little whimpery sound. He kissed her then, taking her mouth in a long, clinging kiss, his hands gently holding her face. Her hands came up and clasped his wrists there, and their mouths connected, a slow, gentle meeting of mouths, tongues nudging, sliding. Her lips were soft and sweet, and he feasted on her mouth, all the feelings he'd been keeping inside pouring into her.

He lifted his mouth from hers, still holding her face,

and rested his forehead against her. "Come on," he muttered. "Let's go to our room."

⬥

They practically ran to their room, hand in hand, Kerri clutching the long skirt of her dress so she wouldn't trip on it in her heels.

Once inside the door, Mitch grabbed her, thrust her up against the wall and kissed her — hard, demanding, urgent.

She pushed at him, but he was so big and heavy, his body crushing her up against the wall and really, she just wanted to kiss him too. Forever. She opened her mouth under his and kissed him back, hot and wet, mouths sliding, tongues swirling. Her hands gripped him and pulled him closer and she felt how hard he was as he thrust his hips forward, grinding against her.

Heat swept over her, dizziness twirled her head and she ached deep inside as the kiss went on and on, hotter and wetter and deeper. She thrust her hands into his hair and gripped tightly, a soft cry escaping her throat.

She gave a little moan, threading her fingers sensuously through his silky hair again as she dissolved between him and the wall.

After he'd kissed her into a puddle on the floor, he picked her up and walked her backward into the hotel room until they fell onto the bed. He came down with her, half lying on her, mouth on hers, hands holding her face, holding her there so he could kiss her more. Her hands moved frantically over his back, clutching him, wanting more of him.

Abruptly, he sat up and yanked the tuxedo jacket off over his arms and tossed it onto the floor. Then he was back on her, kissing the skin on the side of her neck, sucking the soft flesh gently into his mouth, moving lower until he reached the curve where neck met shoulder. He sank his teeth into the muscle there and she cried out.

He reached up and turned on the lamp beside the bed.

"You look so beautiful tonight," he said softly. "Take off that dress."

She rose from the bed and lifted the heavy silk skirt, bunching it in her hands at her waist, and pulled it off over her head. All she wore was a blue thong, the tiny triangle barely covering her curls.

"Now you." She nodded.

His fingers worked to undo the white shirt. It seemed to take forever to get the pearly little studs out. They dropped carelessly to the floor, then he worked on the cuffs. Finally the shirt was off and his chest was bare, smooth and bronze in the soft light. Her mouth filled with saliva and she swallowed.

She ran her hands down her sides and over her belly and his eyes darkened as he watched her. He slid off the bed, unbuttoned, unzipped and stepped out of pants, boxers and socks in a couple of smooth moves.

She stood beside the bed, watching him. He was incredibly beautiful and incredibly aroused, his cock hard and thrusting. "How's my lipstick?" she asked him huskily.

"Huh?"

"My lipstick." She smiled and turned to the mirror over his dresser, touched her mouth. "Danica was right. It did last all day. Let's see how it holds up now."

She dropped to her knees in front of him, taking him in both hands. He cursed softly. She put her mouth on him, just the tip of his penis, sucked softly, then licked him. Her tongue swirled around the head of his cock, then lower down the shaft until she had thoroughly wet him.

"Jesus, Kerri!" His hands slid into her hair, destroying the up-do.

She drew back slightly. "Look at us," she whispered. "Look at yourself fucking my mouth. Tell me what it looks like."

With a groan and heavy eyes, he looked down. Opening wide, she took him in, as much as she could, loving his taste, the feel of him big and velvety in her mouth. She opened her throat and took him deep, swallowing him. He was too big to take all of him, but she tried. "Your lips are all shiny and red and swollen around my cock," he growled, fingers tightening in her hair. "It's so fucking sexy. Kerri...stop..."

She shook her head, sliding her lips up and down him, sucking, using her tongue, wanting him to come in her mouth. She thrilled to know how much pleasure she was giving him. His hips jerked as he thrust in, fucking her mouth. She sucked and drew on him, up and down, cupping his balls with one hand and holding the base of his shaft tightly with the other, until she felt him tighten in her hands, felt his body tense and his hands in her hair threatened to give her bald spots.

With a feeling of exultation, she swallowed the sharp taste as he came in her mouth, sucked him dry, then gently withdrew as she felt the shudders slow. His whole body trembled, and with shaky hands he drew her to her feet and kissed her.

She pressed herself against him, kissing him back with everything she had.

This was it. They'd had sex before and it had been awesome. But tonight was different. Tonight they weren't fuck buddies, or sex pals, or Jack and Jill. Tonight they were lovers in every sense of the word.

His hands were everywhere on her body—her shoulders, her waist, her butt, breasts, hips. Then he lifted her and with a little gasp, she wrapped her legs around him. He pressed his mouth between her breasts and moved to the bed, lowering her gently to the covers.

He looked down at her almost reverently, his eyes dark and hot and intense. She lifted her hands up to his face, wanting to touch him, his cheeks whisker-roughened and hot, and he captured one hand, turning the palm to his mouth to kiss her there, then moving down to her wrist. He pressed a hot, open-mouthed kiss over the pulse there, holding her wrist against his mouth while he slowly breathed in and out, eyes closed.

She couldn't think straight, every nerve in her body tingling and aching. Watching him touch her like that was almost unbearable in its sweetness, its poignancy.

He opened his eyes and they blazed so fiercely she could feel the heat.

He released her hand and she had to touch him, slide her hands over the smooth skin of his broad back, loving the feel of the corded muscles beneath, the heat of him. He lowered his head to her breast and kissed the side of it, the curve underneath, and she moaned, wanting his mouth on her sensitive nipple.

Finally he took her nipple in his mouth, sucking hard, and she shuddered helplessly, making soft little noises. "Don't come yet," he whispered, moving back, his face full of awe at her response to him. "I want you to come with me inside you."

"I want that too. Now, please, Mitch."

He tugged her panties over her hips and legs and tossed them behind him, then reached for a condom in the drawer beside the bed where he must have stashed them earlier. He paused over her, eyes searching for hers again, and when they connected, a web of intimacy enclosed them. He held his penis and pushed into her, gently, withdrawing, then pushing again further, further until he filled her completely. Once in, he reached for her hands and, leaning on his elbows, held her hands beside her head, fingers laced together, bodies joined, gazes fastened on each other.

Tears stung Kerri's eyes at the pure beauty of the moment and she blinked rapidly.

"It's okay, sweetheart. I feel it too." He sighed and

thrust into her slowly, languidly, as if they had all the time in the world.

She lifted against him and after long, luscious moments, he rolled onto his back, taking her with him, still joined. She straddled him, still holding his hands, and leaned down to press kisses to his chest. Then she released his hands to sit up straighter, shaking her hair back as she closed her eyes and rode him.

He slid a hand between them to her clit and stroked it, and she shifted slightly so he could find the perfect spot to rub her. Sliding up and down his shaft, she lifted her hands to her hair, breasts thrust out while sensation spiraled in her, twisting up to an almost unbearable peak.

Flames of pleasure licked over her, hotter, searing her senses. Mitch lifted his other hand to her breast, cupped it, rolled the sensitive nipple between his fingers.

Sensation whipped from nipple to womb and she clenched hard on him inside her. She opened her eyes and gazed down at him, at the masculine pleasure and pain on his face, his eyes dark and hot.

"Come for me, Kerri," he urged hoarsely, watching her. "Come hard."

She shifted again against his fingers and tightened everything inside her as the wave broke, weakness sliding down her legs. "Mitch," she managed to say. "I'm...coming..."

She fell onto him, her body trembling, contracting hard around him, sparkling lights exploding behind her closed lids. Pleasure cascaded over her in wave after wave. Mitch's arms went around her body as he thrust into her one more time and shattered too, pumping into her with long hard, pulses. "God!" he cried, arms tightening almost painfully. "God, Kerri."

They lay like that for a long time, damp and clinging, breathing hard, hearts thudding together.

It was perfect. It was perfectly right, profoundly intimate and intimately connecting.

The tears came then.

"Don't cry, Kerri." Mitch tried to move her hair and lift her face so he could see her. "Please don't cry. You'll make me cry too."

She sniffled a laugh at the idea of big, strong, cynical Mitch crying, and lifted her head. He wiped the tears with his thumbs, tenderly. "I'm sorry."

"Sorry for what?"

"Sorry for crying, to start. It's not an insult to your prowess, believe me."

"A compliment?" he fished, eyes gleaming.

"Definitely a compliment," she assured him. "It's more than that, though. I'm sorry I've been such a bitch."

"God, Kerr, never a bitch. Well, okay, maybe sometimes…"

She smacked him lightly as they both laughed and he pulled her down against him again. She snuggled into his embrace, loving the warmth and strength she felt.

Kerri didn't know how much time had passed—ten minutes? An hour? She had dozed off and woke up in the dark room, plastered against Mitch's hot body. His arms were around her, one hand in her hair, the other on her back. She lifted her head to see if he was awake and found him watching her, a half-smile on his face.

"You always fall asleep after sex." His eyes glinted and the corners of his mouth lifted.

She smiled slowly back at him. "Sorry."

"Hey, it's okay. I don't mind."

"What time is it?"

He glanced at the watch he still wore. "Nearly ten."

"We should go back to the wedding."

"Yeah, we should."

They stayed like that, not moving for a few comfortable, clinging moments, then Kerri moved away and slid out of bed. She looked at her bridesmaid dress in a heap on the floor and grimaced.

"Put on something else," Mitch said. "I am *not* putting that tux back on."

They both found their bags and pulled out the clothes they'd brought for Sunday morning. To their amusement, they were dressed similarly — Mitch in dark jeans and a black T-shirt that stretched across his broad chest and biceps, Kerri also in skinny dark jeans and a ribbed black tank top.

As they approached the entrance to the gazebo, Kerri paused and gripped Mitch's hand with both hers. "People are going to know what we were doing."

21

*M*itch shrugged and pulled her up against him, kissing the top of her head. "Who cares?"

They walked in, hand in hand. The crowd had thinned, most of the remaining guests friends and younger relatives of the bride and groom who were still partying hard, Miguel and Hailey in the thick of things on the crowded dance floor.

Acutely aware of the looks they got as they made their way to a table where their friends were sitting, Kerri caught Hailey's eye and gave a little wave. Hailey immediately deserted her new husband on the dance floor and caught up to Kerri, pulling her back from Mitch. With a smile, Kerri let go of his hand and he slid out two chairs at the table while she hung back to speak to Hailey.

"What the hell?" Hailey asked. "Where'd you two disappear to?"

"Do you really need to ask?" Kerri grinned.

Hailey rolled her eyes. "Kerri…remember what we talked about."

Kerri shook her head, excitement and laughter bubbling up inside her. "It's okay, Hailey. We talked. Oh God, Hailey." She was so happy she couldn't speak for a moment. "Neither of us wants to be friends with benefits. We just want each other."

"Oh." Hailey appeared nonplussed, then grinned broadly. "Oh! So you two are…what? A couple? Exclusive?"

Kerri nodded, her smile matching Hailey's. "Yeah." She sighed. "Oh, yeah."

Hailey smiled even wider, approvingly. "That's so good."

"It is."

Kerri headed to the table where Mitch sat slouched back in his chair, long legs stretched out in front of him, ankles crossed. He was talking to Jason, and as she took the seat beside him, he absently reached for her hand and pulled her close to him.

She couldn't help but smile, knowing she was grinning like an idiot, probably glowing in the dark room like a white shirt under a black light.

⚬⁂⚬

"The guy is so in love with her it's pathetic."

Kerri nodded as she scooped yogurt from the bowl to her mouth. She loved hearing about Mitch's work.

They were sitting in the hotel bed, Mitch cross-legged in his boxer briefs, her naked with the sheet pulled up over her breasts. Mitch had insisted on ordering room service so they could have breakfast in bed.

"She's actually being reasonable about most things," Mitch continued, holding a bagel in one hand. "But she's adamant that they have to keep the dog because the kids love the dog so much."

Kerri nodded. "I guess I can see both points. The kids want the dog and she wants what's best for the kids. But he wants the dog because she's got everything else."

"Yeah. I see both sides too. I told him to get another dog, but that went over like a pregnant pole vaulter." He shook his head as she choked on a laugh. "He's almost ready to let her have the dog because 'he loves her'." His fingers made air quotes.

Kerri smiled sympathetically. "Is there a chance that they might get back together? If he loves her that much..."

Mitch snorted. "He'd be crazy to get back together with her. They'll just end up in the same place down the road."

Kerri sighed. "It is possible for people to work things out sometimes."

"You're a romantic."

"You're cynical."

"I'm realistic."

Kerri shook her head, smiling. They'd had this conversation before. "So how do you help this guy? You don't tell him he'd be crazy to try again, do you?"

He shrugged. "No, I don't tell him that, despite what I think. I just try to represent his interests. The poor bastard."

She reached for the other half of the bagel on Mitch's plate. "Hey." He grabbed her hand and held her away from his food. "Mine."

She laughed, and fought him. He grinned, trying to keep her away, but when he had to choose between hurting her or losing his food...well, the bagel fell onto the bed and he fell onto her, both of them laughing. His kissed her, hot, wet, with tongue, and he tasted like coffee and cream cheese and sin.

"Okay, never mind the bagels." She gasped as his mouth moved to her throat. He sucked there and she laughed again. "Don't! I don't want love bites all over my neck! What will my students think?"

He grinned evilly and lowered his head again to her. She pushed at him and they rolled together across the bed, over the bagels, the empty yogurt bowl thudding to the carpeted floor. He let her put up a fight, but really it was so easy for him to pin her down, holding her hands over her head so he could kiss her mouth, her throat, her breasts, and then she wasn't fighting him anymore, she was moaning and begging for more.

She couldn't believe how many times they'd made love. It was like they couldn't get enough of each other, or were making up for lost time. Even looking at him now made her weak and wet.

When she stopped struggling, he let down his guard, and with a quick hard push she was able to toss him to his back and climb onto him, straddling him, grinning. "Ha. Now I'm on top."

He grinned back. "Oh no. Please be gentle with me."

She paused, gazing at him below her, all sleek muscles and bronze skin, mussed hair and faint shadowy beard darkening his face. Molten pleasure slid through her, and she closed her eyes briefly. She leaned down to kiss his nipples, flicking her tongue over them, making him groan. Daringly, she took a tight nipple between her teeth, scraped it gently, and he shuddered beneath her.

She nibbled her way down his abs to the top of his briefs, then buried her face between his legs, inhaling deeply. "God you smell good." She breathed in his male and musky scent. She kissed his erection through the cotton, stretched tautly across his thick length.

She used her hands to push his thighs apart so she could slip her hands inside the leg opening of the briefs and cup him, her face still pressed there, feeling his heat, breathing in his scent.

"Kerri," he said weakly. "You're killing me."

"No, I'm not." She sat up, pulling her hands out of his underwear. He groaned again. "Oh, you *didn't* want me to stop?"

He muttered something unintelligible. She loved, *loved* how she could affect him like this. He was so hard, leaking a little bit, dampening his briefs, and she touched him there, right on the head of his cock. She looked at his face, his eyes squeezed closed, jaw locked.

She ran her fingers over and around the head, through the cotton, gauging his reaction. His tongue came out to lick his lips and he swelled even bigger and harder in her hand.

"What do you want, Mitch?" she asked, her voice husky. "Do you want to come inside me again? Or do you want to come in my mouth?"

"Jesus," he croaked. "Kerri…"

"Mmm? Tell me what you want." Her fingers continued to tease him.

He apparently could not answer. "Okay, I'll decide for you. You smell so good, I want to taste you. I want to suck on you."

"Jesus," he muttered again, his face flushed.

She yanked his underwear off and he lifted his legs to help her get rid of them. His erection rose up, dark and hard and oozing, and her breath caught at how beautiful he was. She took him in her hands and bent her head to him to lick the drops there, savoring his taste.

His hands came to her head, fisted in her hair, and it almost hurt, but she loved it. As she closed her mouth around his cock, he pulled harder and she almost disintegrated into a puddle of hungry lust. She sucked on him, swirled her tongue around him, eliciting more curses and groans.

God, she loved doing this to him, loved the taste of him, the smell of him, the way she could make him shudder and twitch. After, his arms went around her and held her tightly to him as he recovered. A while later he said, "I really don't want to know how you got to be so good at that."

She smiled against his chest.

CXIXCO

"Okay, I have to talk about this." Kerri found Sela in her office the next day.

"About what? The wedding?" Sela didn't look up from her computer monitor.

"No, not the wedding. Me and Mitch." Kerri sighed happily.

Sela's gaze snapped up to Kerri's face. "What about you and Mitch?"

"We're…well, what are we? Um…we're seeing each other."

"Well. It's about time."

Kerri laughed, a little disappointed in the reaction. She'd expected more surprise. She put her hands to her cheeks.

"I've been so stupid. He's the guy I've been looking for and all along he was right there in front of me."

Sela smiled. "I'm so happy for you two. I'm glad you finally figured it out."

"Me too."

Not only had the sex been mind-blowing, it had been fun. She'd never had so much fun and laughed so much in bed. In fact, she wasn't sure if she'd ever laughed in bed with a man. Well, that time Grant Bedford had removed the condom too fast and snapped a very sensitive area had been funny. Although, to him, not so much.

She and Mitch knew each other so well. They could talk about anything and laugh at everything. They'd eaten in bed, laughed in bed, made love in bed. She got that warm, squishy feeling deep inside again. God, she was pathetic. She grinned.

"I guess you won't be getting much work done today." Sela grinned.

Kerri wandered into her office still smiling. What to do, what to do. She shuffled some papers, then worked on the website. Neta's photographs made the spa look awesome, as well as her beautiful new yoga studio. This *had* to increase business, with all the services clearly displayed — prices, hours of operation, her class schedule.

It would be interesting to see the hits on it once it was up and running.

To her surprise, the day passed quickly and she actually accomplished a lot. More than she had the last few weeks when she'd been so confused and miserable.

Her mother phoned that night to invite her for dinner on the weekend and she happily accepted. "Can I bring Mitch?"

"Of course," her mother said. "Why do you sound funny? What's going on?"

"Mitch and I are…um…together."

There was stunned silence, then, "Oh my God! Kerri, that's wonderful!"

Kerri laughed. "Yeah. It is."

"How did this happen? You know, I was watching you two at your party, and I said to your dad, Scott, something is wrong between those two, they're not acting like they usually do."

"I guess we've been kind of fighting our feelings for each other for a while, and ended up fighting with each other." Kerri sighed. "But things are good now."

"He's such an amazing young man. I am so happy for both of you, and I can't wait to see you."

When Mitch called, just to talk, she told him about the conversation with her mother and he laughed. "She likes me," he said smugly.

"Yes, she does." She rolled her eyes. "The last time we were there she was making comments about us. And then at the grand opening party I overheard Sela and Hailey talking about us and how we were crazy about each other and didn't know it."

"*I* knew it."

She melted all over again but said, "Arrogant much?"

His low laugh warmed her heart.

"I'm sorry I was such an idiot. Apparently everybody else knew we should be together."

"You're not an idiot. Tell me about your day."

When they went over to her parents' home for dinner that weekend, after seeing each other, or at least talking to each other every day, Kerri wrestled with nerves—would her parents make a big fuss about them? Would it feel weird? But no. They were just as warm and welcoming to Mitch as ever, and didn't ask any embarrassing personal questions at all. As they sat outside on the patio eating dinner, relief shimmered through her. She watched Mitch talk, so smart and articulate, and love and admiration warmed her insides.

"You look like you're in love," her mother said to her in the kitchen in a private moment.

"I think I am." Kerri's heart gave an extra beat. Oh lord. "I just can't believe it took me this long to realize it."

"And does Mitch feel the same?"

"I…think so."

Mom smiled at her fondly. "You seem so happy, I love to see that." She gave Kerri a quick hug before they took dessert outside to the others.

22

"My dad is bringing his new girlfriend to town to meet me," Mitch told Kerri with disgust a week later.

"That's nice. Isn't it?"

He shook his head violently. They sat in her living room, about to watch a Netflix movie. "He just split up with his last wife. Honestly, the ink probably isn't even dry on the divorce papers. And now he has someone new."

"He doesn't like to be alone, does he?"

He looked at Kerri. "You think that's what it is?"

"I have no idea." She shrugged, crossing her legs into the lotus position on the couch. "I don't even know him. It just sounds like it."

"I guess I can understand that, but why can't his relationships last? And knowing he doesn't have a good track record, why would he bother to keep getting married over and over again? Just live together or something, for God's sake."

"Marriage must mean something to him."

"It means another alimony payment. Thank God he's never had more kids. That would get really expensive." He glanced at her. "He wants to meet you, too. But you don't have to, if you don't want. Believe me, he's no treat."

"He's your father."

"I know, but I just…I don't exactly *hate* him…"

"Mitch! You can't hate your father."

"Kerri, Kerri, you've led such a sheltered life." He slid his arm around her and pulled her close, tugging her off balance in her cross-legged position. With a giggle she righted herself and snuggled into him. "I said I don't hate him. I just have no respect for him. It's such a loser way to keep living your life."

"Of course I'll meet him," she said softly. "Maybe I won't like him either, but he is your dad."

⟳〲⟲

Two days later, when Jeff MacAulay introduced Mitch and Kerri to a visibly pregnant young woman with short curly brown hair, Kerri felt Mitch cringe as his words came back to smack him in the face. "This is Carmen," Jeff said, and Mitch avoided her eyes as they shook hands and murmured greetings. When they took their seats, Kerri laid her hand on Mitch's leg under the table and dug her fingers in to his rigid muscles.

"So Mitch, how's work going? That big-shot law career still going well?"

Kerri could hear the pride in Jeff's voice despite the casually worded question. She studied Mitch's dad. In looks, they were very similar—tall, broad, handsome. Jeff had the same casual charm and easy smile. It was hard not to like him.

They made small talk, Mitch talking very briefly about his move into collaborative law. Then Mitch started asking Carmen about herself. Kerri felt the waves of hostility and tension coming off him and wondered if the others sensed it too. Carmen seemed very friendly, almost naïve, and oblivious to any undercurrents. She also seemed very young, younger than both Kerri and Mitch. Holy smokes.

"So, guess what." Jeff smiled broadly. "Carmen and I are getting married."

"No shit," Mitch muttered.

Kerri grabbed his hand and squeezed.

Jeff frowned. "Hey. Congratulate us. You should be happy for us."

"Congratulations," Mitch said shortly. "When is the wedding?"

"Actually we're thinking of this weekend."

Mitch choked on his drink.

"Well, maybe you didn't notice, but Carmen is expecting," Jeff continued happily. "You're going to have a brother or sister, Mitch."

"Congratulations," he managed to sputter again. "Wow."

"When are you due?" Kerri asked Carmen softly.

"Right around Christmas." She smiled gently. "It's going to be awesome." She paused. "We would love for you two to be at the wedding."

Mitch was clearly struggling for words. "Um…"

"Mitch is a busy guy," his father said quietly. "And he doesn't much like weddings."

⟡

"I don't like *his* weddings," Mitch snorted later, sitting in his SUV in front of Kerri's condo.

"I'm sorry."

"Hey, don't be sorry. That's just the way he is. I can't believe he's going to do it again."

"It's his life, Mitch."

"Ha. It *was* his life. Now he's having another kid. Jesus Christ." He thrust a hand through his hair. "I wonder if my mom knows about this. She must be killing herself laughing."

Mitch's family was certainly unique. Which was why he'd been so determined to remain single. Was he worried he was going to end up like his father, with multiple divorces yet pathetically afraid to be alone? It wasn't surprising that he had some odd ideas about marriage.

"My stepmother is younger than I am," he said. "And I'm going to have a brother or sister young enough to be my own kid. That's just sick."

Kerri set a hand on his back and rubbed it up and down. "Well, it's unusual." She felt some tension release in his muscles. "You need to spend more time with my family. So you can see what a real marriage is like." He gave her a look and she smiled at him. "Seriously. My mom and dad will adopt you. They love you."

He laughed. "Hey, I love them too. And I've seen their marriage, and believe me, it's not like my family." He smiled at her, and she could tell he was calmer and more accepting of his father's choices. "You got a class tomorrow?"

"Yes. My kids' class. At ten o'clock."

He hesitated. "You want sleep? Or can I come in?"

Sleep? Who needed sleep? "Come in."

Later, they lay in bed, her head on his chest, hands stroking him, his fingers tracing little patterns on her shoulder. "What happened with all that oil you made?" he asked idly. "Did Sela find out about it?"

"God no. But Amanda loves it. She's been using it on her clients. She tried the ginger oil on a couple of guys who'd just run a triathlon and they swore it helped. She says the lavender one almost puts people to sleep, it's so relaxing. She wants more."

"Jesus. You'll have to open a factory."

She laughed. "That's a good idea. Then I could try all

the other ideas I have for skin care—cleansers, scrubs—all natural stuff that makes you feel good and look good."

"You sound like an entrepreneur."

She lifted her shoulder a little. "I *am* a businesswoman. Nobody ever seems to recognize that."

"Hey." He sounded surprised. "What are you talking about?"

She concentrated on his chest. "My parents think Sela is the businesswoman in the family. She's so successful, making mega bucks, plus she has a husband and kids. She's superwoman. She can do it all. On the other hand, I have some little yoga thing that I play around with. They don't take me seriously at all." She tried not to sound too bitter.

"I'm sure that's not true. I know your parents are proud of you."

"Even you," she continued accusingly. "You're always so impressed with Sela."

"I am not!"

"Yes, you are!"

"Well, I do admire her success, but that doesn't take away from anything you've done. You're a great businesswoman, Kerri. Even with all that flaky woo woo new age stuff."

She gave a little gasp of laughter. "Flaky! I am *so* not flaky." But his compliment warmed her, surprised her.

He laughed too. "I know you're not deep down, but sometimes you seem that way when you start talking about chakras and transfiguration and spiritual fulfillment."

"Well. I'll show you. I've been studying up on some things and you're going to love it."

"Hmmm. Now you've got me intrigued."

"Saturday night. Be ready."

"You have to tell me what it is. You can't just drop that little teaser and leave me hanging."

"Oh yes I can. The anticipation is all part of it." She grinned. She'd had the idea for a while, but didn't know exactly when she was going to do it. Saturday night they planned to go out for dinner and then see a movie or something after. So this would be the "or something".

❦

Mitch had made dinner reservations at a romantic restaurant just off Alameda Padre Serra. In a small hotel set in lush, tropical grounds, the patio overlooked the lights of the city. Glowing candles and lamps cast the foliage into shadows and created a dreamy, seductive ambience.

"This is so beautiful." Kerri gazed around.

An attentive waiter handed them menus. Kerri studied the tantalizing selections while Mitch ordered a bottle of Pinot Grigio.

"I was debating between here and Insatiable," he said. "Have you ever been there?"

"No, but I hear it's amazing. Super expensive, though."

"Yeah, but one of the best restaurants in the country. But I decided here was quieter. Insatiable is a place for people watching. Apparently Oprah likes to eat there."

Kerri grinned. "Yeah, that's my kind of place. Oprah and me, we go way back."

He laughed and sipped his wine, watching her across the table. The hint of a breeze stirred her glossy black hair. Her eyes sparkled in the candlelight and he couldn't remember ever seeing her look so happy or so beautiful. Christ, he was lucky.

"So what are we going to do after dinner? You told me to be ready. I'm thinking you don't have a movie in mind."

She smiled slowly. "It's nothing, really. Tell me what's happening at work this week."

Amused by her deflection and although intensely curious, he went along with her conversational lead.

Their food arrived, beautifully presented and delicious.

"Don't eat too much," Kerri warned him.

Hmm. What did she have in store for them? "Are we going swimming?" he asked, half serious, half teasing.

She shook her head and touched her napkin to her mouth.

After dinner, they shared a decadent mocha dessert and lingered over strong, smooth coffee.

Mitch glanced at his watch. "Do we need to leave?"

"Just stop trying to get me to tell you!" She laughed. "We can leave anytime. But on our way, I need to stop at the spa."

"Oh. Okay." Saturday night the place was closed. Did she need to pick up something?

Kerri needed to use the ladies' room as they left the restaurant, so he pulled the car around and waited for her at the entrance. She slipped in moments later.

He drove leisurely through the dark streets, down State, turning on Chapala and parking in front of the studio. "Should I just wait here?"

"No, come in. I'll be a few minutes."

She opened the front door and they stepped into the salon. Just as Kerri locked the door behind them, Mitch thought he heard another door closing—at the back of the salon. Huh?

"Come with me." She led the way down the hall.

Mitch noticed lights coming from the yoga studio and the thought entered his head that Kerri must have left them on for security. But when he reached the French doors into the large room, he stopped.

Candles arranged along the front wall of the studio cast a warm, wavery glow across the dark room.

"What the…"

Kerri crossed over to the small desk where the sound

system sat and dropped her little purse there. She pressed a button on the stereo and slow, soft piano music drifted across the room. She slipped out of the little cardigan she wore over her dress.

"Come in," she invited him softly.

"What are we doing?" he asked stupidly. His jaw dropped as she reached behind her to unzip her dress and then slid it down over her shoulders, arms, hips until it floated to the floor at her feet.

"This is your fantasy."

23

S he stood in nothing but a pink lace bra and matching boy-short panties, looking ethereal in the candlelight. Slowly, she put her palms together in front of her chest and drew one foot up her leg, standing in the tree pose, her eyes never leaving his face. Her balance was exquisite.

He moved toward her as if in a dream, inhaling a scent that made him light-headed. Drunk. He closed his hands around her bare waist. "What..." He tried again.

She lowered her foot gracefully to the floor and started unbuttoning his shirt. "Remember? You told me your ultimate fantasy was naked yoga. So that's what we're going to do."

He gulped.

"I know there isn't a whole class of naked people doing yoga, but I thought that might be a bit hard to arrange. So it's just you and me. I hope that's okay."

He couldn't get a word out. She was slowly pulling his shirt out of his pants and down over his arms, all the while pressing little kisses to his face. She tossed the shirt aside and went to work on his pants.

Her fingers teased the skin of his lower abdomen as she felt around for the button of his pants. She brushed over the fly, now straining with his hard-on, then moved back to his bare stomach, which quivered under her fingers. With measured, deliberate moves, she flicked the fastener open, then slid the zipper of his fly down tooth by tantalizing tooth.

He gritted his teeth against the desire to rip his pants off.

After long, luxurious moments, he was naked and she gave him her back so he could unclasp her bra. She let it fall off, and shimmied out of the panties. Taking his hand, she led him slowly to the centre of the room where a large yoga mat had been placed. Beside it sat a bottle of what looked like her oil, a fleece blanket and several cushions.

"We're going to do the V letter," she told him softly. "Hold my wrists." They clasped each others' wrists. "Now, lean back." She leaned away from him, pulling their arms out straight, and he did the same. "Arch your back." Her head fell back. "Feel the point where we're perfectly balanced." He held on, letting his head drop back although all he really wanted to do was look at her luscious breasts thrust forward by the pose.

"Focus on the energetic exchanges occurring through the arms," she said. "Feel the activation of Swadhistana chakra, the capacity of having highly erotic feelings."

Well, it felt good. And yes...erotic.

"Now, come out of it slowly." Together they pulled themselves up, and damned if they weren't perfectly balanced, coming up together in one smooth, graceful movement.

"Cool," he said.

She smiled.

"Bend your knees." Together they lowered their bodies, this time looking at each other, eyes locked. "This brings harmony, trust and intimacy to the relationship. Notice how your ability to balance is determined by me, and my ability to balance is determined by you. The longer we can maintain this pose, the greater the harmony between us. This pose will help us have a highly erotic experience."

"I'm good with that."

"Now, kneel down." Together they lowered themselves to the mat, kneeling in front of each other. She slid her hands up his arms to just below his elbows. "Hold me like this, too," she requested. "This is ustrasana. It will help us experience a state of euphoria and empathy. Now lean back..." She leaned away from him, her head falling back, her hands holding his arms as their arms straightened and pulled. He followed her lead. "Relax your neck," she murmured. "Feel the free circulation of the energies through our arms and the activation of the solar plexus. Feel the inner state of euphoria."

He wasn't sure if he was feeling euphoria. More likely, he was feeling light-headed from lack of blood, all the blood in his body racing to his rock-hard dick.

"Sit down," she commanded softly, lowering herself in a fluid move onto the blanket into the lotus position. She tugged on his hand and he bent his knees and sat down with a bit of thud, much less gracefully than her.

"Cross your legs, like me." She still held his hands. Feeling awkward, he shifted his legs and crossed them, supremely conscious of his hard cock thrusting out aggressively and on display between his legs. Kerri's gaze lowered there briefly, admiringly, then she gazed back at him with a serene but warm expression.

His own gaze went between her legs. She sat there completely spread open to him, all pink and pretty, and he had to swallow hard. His cock jumped.

She took his other hand and they sat there in the flickering candle light, soft music flowing around them, the scent of something incredibly erotic mingling with the scent of Kerri's arousal.

"What is that scent?"

"Jasmine. It's an aphrodisiac. It's a love plant, used for

love spells. In India the jasmine flower symbolizes the promise of eternal love." Her words were soft, seductive. "Tantra is the ancient art of prolonging the pleasure of lovemaking up to reaching a superior level of consciousness. In other words, you delay the usual way of experiencing orgasm, taking time to fully live and enjoy each sensation, each thrill that crosses your body."

"How long do I have to wait?" he asked uneasily.

She smiled slowly, breathtakingly. "The idea is, if you maintain a high level of sexual excitement without rushing to the end, involve all your senses in the experience, slowly and patiently let the intensity grow, your attention is focused on the whole path of your sensual journey. Not just the destination. If you get what I mean."

She tilted her head just slightly as gazed at him, her eyes hot and intent.

"I get it," he said hoarsely.

"We're going to breathe together. Do you remember how to do yogic breathing?"

"Uh...I think so."

"Breathe in...through the nostrils...fill your belly..." She instructed as they went, her voice low and velvety.

He followed her directions, feeling just a little silly, but he went along with it.

"We're going to breathe in unison," she whispered. Her eyes focused steady and warm on his face as they inhaled slowly, exhaled even slower, again and again. After only a few breaths, Mitch felt his body relaxing...well, most of his body. His cock got even harder, if that was possible.

There was something about breathing with Kerri that made him feel...weird. Not bad weird, but good weird. Mesmerized. Hypnotized. His chest rose and, although he kept his eyes on her face, he could sense her breasts rising at the same time. The movements of their bodies were slight but synchronized, and a feeling of peace flowed slowly over him.

His gaze locked with hers and he had the fantastic thought that he could see inside her soul as their breaths mingled and their bodies moved together. He had no idea how long they sat there and breathed together, but when Kerri let go of his hands and gently placed her palms on his face, he felt as if he was in a trance.

Her warm soft hands framed his face, her eyes still on his. "I'm going to touch you all over," she whispered. "I made a special oil just for us."

She reached carefully for the bottle that sat beside them and poured a generous amount into her hand. Again, the scent went straight to his dick. It wasn't a strong smell, but had a distinct effect on him.

She laid her hands on his shoulders and rubbed them over him, so agonizingly slowly, stroking softly, lushly. She moved from there down his arms, over his biceps that flexed under her touch. A small, admiring smile touched her lips as she stroked him, watched every muscle bunch and twitch. "Relax," she whispered.

"You have got to be kidding me. I am so far from relaxed..."

"But you're enjoying it...aren't you?" A notch appeared between her eyebrows.

"Christ, yeah." He groaned with pleasure as her hands, slick with the oil, found his again. It was only his *hands*, for God's sake, but as she rubbed and slid her fingers over and between his, he felt it through every cell of his body. Pleasure surged through his veins, sensations sparked across his flesh and he ached for her. "I don't know if I can do this. God, Kerri, I need you so bad."

"I know. You can do it. Just feel every sensation. Enjoy every touch. Don't think too far ahead."

He closed his eyes, his head feeling heavy on his shoulders, and his world narrowed to Kerri's hands on him, everywhere, teasing, touching, tempting. An erotic cocoon of soft music, exotic scents and enticing touch enclosed them. It could have been hours later when Kerri finally broke the spell, his whole body burning up, a mass of sizzling erotic sensations.

"Now it's your turn," he dimly heard her say over the blood roaring in his ears. Her hands rested on his knees. She had touched him everywhere except where he really, really wanted to her to touch. He almost groaned again.

He struggled to open his eyes. She sat in front of him, and to his lust-fogged eyes she appeared to have a glowing aura around her nude body. He blinked.

She took his hand, turned it palm up, and poured some of the oil into it. It almost felt burning hot, which was very strange. He rubbed his hands together as she had, feeling the warmth seep through his already heated body.

He touched her shoulders almost hesitantly, feeling a little overwhelmed by the intensity of the experience. Some kind of weird shit was going on here.

Her shoulders were so small and smooth. He smoothed his hands over them, trying to go slowly. His hands wanted to race to her breasts, but he resisted.

"Keep concentrating on the sensation," she breathed. "This part is still for you, too."

"Yeah." He followed the same path over her body as she had over his, her firm, slender arms, her small hands. When he took her hands in his and slipped his fingers between hers, slick and warm from the oil, he felt as if some kind of energy passed between them. He almost jerked back at the force of it.

Startled, he met her eyes and she, too, looked a bit unnerved, blinking rapidly.

He swallowed and kept going, from her small toes, up sleek legs, focusing intently on keeping his touch slow and lingering. Her eyes, too, fell closed as she drank in the sounds and scents and absorbed his touch.

His hands hovered over her breasts, aching to fill his palms with her lush softness.

She opened her eyes and reached up for his hands. "Not yet."

God! He almost fell over onto his back. "I'm gonna die, Kerri."

She shook her head. "No you aren't."

She poured more oil into her palm and on the back of her hand and touched his cock. Her fingers delicately and excitingly touched his scrotum, then massaged his testicles with both hands. The top of his head was going to blow off and his skin tightened and prickled all over. His thighs went rigid and pressure built at the base of his spine, agonizingly sweet. His whole body was aroused to such a heightened point of sensitivity he feared he might explode.

"Okay, now you can touch me like that."

Eagerly, but trying to go slowly, he reached out and slid his slick fingers into her folds, gently, teasingly parting her, tracing her crevice up, then down.

He flinched when she reached back to him, delicately squeezing the base of his cock with one hand, keeping it away from the rest of his body. She formed a circle around the head with the fingers of her other hand, rotated her fingers clockwise, one finger sliding away from the head of the penis over and over again until he gasped. Sensation exploded through him and he fought for control.

"Keep touching me," she whispered and again he tried to focus, blinking rapidly and swallowing hard. "Touch me inside." While he pushed two fingers slickly inside her, his other hand pressed on her clitoris. "Oh!"

"Are you going to come, Kerr?"

"No," she rasped. "Yes...no, not yet, not yet..."

"Do you want me to stop?"

She gave a little nod and reluctantly he drew his hands away, slippery with the oil and her cream.

Her hands withdrew from his cock as well, and she rested them on his knees. He covered her hands with his while they both drew in long, dragging breaths. His lungs had seized up.

"We need to breathe together again."

Their eyes met again and Mitch used every ounce of control he had to pull in a long, slow breath, matching his rhythm to hers until they were back in that trance-like state. His skin was on fire, every nerve in his body stretched and sensitized, his senses acutely aware of the feel of Kerri's hands beneath his, her chest rising in unison with his, the soft sounds of their breathing.

Their gazes locked together again and he couldn't have looked away from her if someone put a gun to his head. His fingers tightened reflexively on hers.

"Now," she breathed. She reached to the side, straightened and handed him a condom. "I'm going to spontaneously combust if you don't make me come."

"God, yes," he groaned. He rolled on the condom. Although he wanted to pleasure her instantly, he felt as if he was moving in slow motion, his fingers unable to hurry. He touched her again, found her moisture, slicked it over her folds, sought her swollen clit. His fingers had barely brushed over it when she came in hard shuddering waves, her head falling forward.

"God!" Her hand turned in his and gripped him so tightly he was afraid she was breaking bones. "Oh, God," she said again, moments later, lifting her head. He had never seen her look like that...her face glowed, here eyes shone, her mouth curved into a sinful smile. "Stretch your legs out," she directed him gently, and he did so. She crawled onto his lap, sliding her arms around his neck, and he held her waist. She positioned herself over him, then lowered herself onto him, and Christ it felt incredible. His cock was so super-sensitized and engorged he'd been almost afraid the condom wouldn't fit over it.

She moved on him, their faces level, watching each other. He shook his head slightly. "I can't wait."

"It's okay. I'm…" She bit her lip, shifted her position ever so slightly. "I'm already…there…" She came again, little convulsions that gripped his cock like a fist, milking him, and the sight of her face in ecstasy and the feel of her contracting around him sent him over the edge. He came, wave after wave of heat rippling over him, shuddering violently in a tumultuous, exploding climax like he had never experienced.

Shimmering lights danced before his eyes, and he held on to Kerri tighter, clasping her small waist as she too pulsed and throbbed.

When he could open his eyes, Kerri was looking at him and he was back in that trance-like state where they were breathing as one, moving as one, connected, merged into an extraordinary erotic and psychic fusion.

Holy shit.

"I'm sorry I called you flaky," he choked out. "I take it back."

24

Kerri smiled at him, and something ached in his chest. She was stunning, absolutely, incredibly stunning. "All our actions and thoughts originate in love, drawing us toward a divine center of irresistible attraction. Yoga is a path of knowledge, a path of love and loving." She paused, her gaze fastened on his. "I love you, Mitch."

"I love you too." He pulled her closer, needed to hug her tightly to him, still joined together at their centers. He never wanted to let her go. "I love you so much, I can't even tell you."

They stayed like that for a long time, then Kerri said, "The last part of the yoga workout is a nice warm shower. Whenever you're ready, we can go upstairs."

"We're going to have a shower? Together?"

"Mmmm. The shower in the spa is used for some of the treatments. It's nice and big and there's a bench in there to sit on."

"Oh Christ." He took in a long, deep breath. "Give me a minute."

She reached for the blanket and cushions, dragging them closer. She wrapped the blanket around the two of them, pushed him down to the mat and, snuggled into him, tucking a pillow under her head more comfortably. "Whenever you're ready," she repeated.

This was *way* better than his fantasy. He'd had no idea that the things she would do would reach so far inside him that they would connect like that. His fantasy had involved physical movements, the visual stimulation of seeing her body, the carnality of touching her and her touching him. The reality had fulfilled that beyond his wildest dreams. But the spirituality, the emotions she'd evoked in him as their eyes had met and held, as their breathing connected and merged, was not something he had ever contemplated or even known was possible. His stomach still quivered with the emotional overload. What had she done to him?

He might have drifted off to sleep or maybe he was in another trance, when Kerri moved in his arms.

"We should go shower now," she murmured. "As nice as this was, we don't want to spend all night here."

He smiled his agreement and helped her blow out the candles before they went upstairs. She turned on lights as they went, only enough for them to see where they were going, until they arrived in the treatment room. Tiny pot lights around the perimeter of the room provided warm, subdued lighting. She turned on the water to let it heat up and reached for two thick towels from a shelf.

She must have planned ahead for this, too, because a bottle of some kind of aromatherapy shower gel sat in the shower. She dumped some into her hands and spread it over his chest, his shoulders, her hands sliding easily over him with the thick, smooth liquid. The scent alone was arousing, but her hands slick on his body almost undid him.

"My turn," he groaned, grabbing the bottle, and he washed her, too, over smooth curves and dips. Her head fell back with enjoyment, and he slid his fingers between her legs.

"Yes," she whispered, the water showering warmly down on them. He moved his fingers there, caressing, stroking. She grabbed the bottle of gel and dumped more into his hand so they didn't lose the slickness of the gel in the water spraying down on them. Then she came, and he had to hold her up as her legs threatened to give way.

He lowered her onto the marble bench, a shower head in the wall behind her keeping her wet and warm.

She opened her eyes, deep blue and framed with spiky wet lashes, She reached again for the bottle, poured gel into her hands, took his hard cock in her hands and stroked, the gel lubricating him and intensifying the sensations until he thought he might burst.

"Harder," he muttered, bracing his arms on the wall, muscles and tendons taut. She increased the pressure and he felt the tingle starting, building. His head dropped back, he gritted his teeth as his orgasm erupted through him, almost as intense as the one she'd drawn from him downstairs. His hot semen spilled over her hands, the water washing it away as her hands slowed and gentled on him.

He collapsed on the bench beside her, and pulled her against him, burying his face in her wet hair.

"Okay, you have succeeded," he wheezed, sucking air into his lungs.

"Succeeded at what?" she asked lazily, curling into him.

"You have made me your love slave. I know that was your intention. You've used some magic karma or something."

She giggled and stroked his wet chest. "The only problem is, I seem to have succumbed to the same magic charm because I think I'm your slave too. Whatever you want, whenever you want."

Her words sent a shiver through his exhausted, sated

body and he wasn't entirely sure if it was fear or excitement…or both.

Hailey called as soon as she and Miguel were back from their honeymoon in Paris, inviting Kerri and Mitch and some other friends over to see their pictures and all the clothes she had bought.

They went over Saturday night and Kerri hugged her friend. "I missed you."

"How are things with Mitch?" Hailey asked urgently. "I couldn't stop thinking about you two the whole time."

"Hopefully not the whole time." Kerri smiled. "You *were* on your honeymoon, after all."

Hailey waved a hand. "Miguel and I have been together for six years." Then she grinned. "Okay, I wasn't thinking about you the *whole* time."

"Things are awesome," Kerri said dreamily. "I love him so much."

Hailey's eyes widened. "Whoa! Have you told him that?"

She nodded happily. "Yeah. He loves me too. I can't believe this is happening."

Hailey looked at her, shaking her head almost as if she couldn't believe it herself, but smiling. "Wow."

"Yeah. Wow."

They joined the others and pored over all the pictures Hailey and Miguel had taken displayed on Miguel's laptop.

"It looks so beautiful." Kerri sighed. "You're so lucky."

"Also lucky to be a teacher and have two months of holidays in the summer," Mitch said.

"I know," Hailey answered. "Back to school next week, though. Classes don't start until the week after, but I have to go in and get things ready. I can't believe summer's almost over."

"It's been a great summer." Kerri gave another happy sigh and exchanged a smile with Mitch.

After they'd made love that night, Kerri curled into Mitch's side and petted his chest.

"Let's go to Paris," he said.

She lifted her head, stunned. "Huh?"

He smiled and stroked her hair. "We should go. You want to go. When's the last time you took a holiday?"

"Ha. I don't even remember."

"Exactly. But now you have people who could take over your classes, and Sela could cover for you for a week if we went away, couldn't she?"

Kerri considered that. "I suppose she could." Excitement bubbled in her. "Really? You really mean it?"

He nodded. "I'd love to take you to Paris. So let's go."

"Oh my God!" That was so incredibly exciting! Then she had a thought. "But maybe we should wait."

"Wait for what?" His hand still idly stroked her hair.

"We should save Paris. Save it for our honeymoon."

His hand stilled. She felt his body tense beneath her, and the temperature in the room dropped several chilling degrees.

Kerri's stomach tightened and she lifted her head. "What?"

"Honeymoon?" He shook his head slightly, gently moving her off him to the side. She flipped over and sat up, pulling the covers over her naked breasts, still tender and swollen from his earlier attentions.

She stared at him, sensing something really bad but not sure exactly what. Her fingers shook and her stomach churned. "Yeah. What...what's wrong with that?"

He closed his eyes. "Kerri. You know I don't believe in marriage."

She took that in and turned it over in her mind. "But

that was before. Before...us. Before we fell in love."

Eyes still closed, he sat up and leaned back against the headboard. He rubbed his face with both hands, then opened his eyes and looked up at the ceiling. "That doesn't change how I feel about marriage," he said flatly. "It's still a mistake."

She stared at him in stunned disbelief. How could he say that? Yes, she knew what he thought about marriage, but she'd been sure that now he'd fallen in love—or so he said—he would of course want to get married. Wasn't that the next natural step in a relationship? She'd thought maybe they would move in together first, but she assumed that if they loved each other they'd get married. One day.

Oh God.

Her stomach tightened painfully and her heart thudded.

"Mitch." She reached out and put a hand on his forearm. It was hard as a rock. "You can't mean that. Not now."

He ran a hand through his hair, clearly disturbed by the conversation. "I don't really want to talk about this," he growled. "We've talked about this before and we've agreed to disagree. Marriage is not in my future. Not ever."

Her heart squeezed painfully. "No. But...what about me?"

He looked at her. "What about you? I thought you loved me. Isn't that enough?"

She shook her head slowly, her head spinning. This could not be happening. She clutched the sheet tighter in her hands. "I want to get married. You knew that. I want a family. I want kids."

He just looked back at her, his face grim.

"No," she whispered, head whirling. "No, don't do this to me, Mitch. We finally found each other. I finally found the man I want to spend the rest of my life with and you're telling me you won't marry me?"

"The rest of your life is a long time," Mitch said cautiously. "You can't know that you want to spend the rest of your life with someone. That never happens."

"It does happen!" She scrambled out of the bed, pulling the sheet with her. She stood staring at him. *That never happens?* Obviously he didn't picture the two of them together for long. When he said nothing, her heart contracted sharply as if it were actually breaking. "No," she whispered again.

After another long moment heavy with unspoken disappointment and sorrow, Kerri turned to look for her clothes, almost blind with grief. She felt around and almost by touch alone found her underwear. She set it aside and pulled on her jeans and T-shirt, stuffed the panties in her pocket. Her hands shook so much she almost couldn't button her jeans.

"Kerri, what are you doing?" Mitch snapped. "Don't go."

She snorted. "You expect me to *stay*?" Her throat ached and her stomach tightened painfully. She shoved her feet into her flip flops and stumbled out of the bedroom. She found her purse and dug for her keys. Shit. She had no way to get home.

She grabbed his keys off the table near his front door and slammed out. She hurried to his SUV, in a panic that he would follow her and try to stop her, almost unable to get the key into the ignition with her trembling hands. The engine roared as she started it and put it in gear, just as Mitch emerged from the front door, having pulled on a pair of boxers. He stood there as she squealed out of his driveway and up the street.

She had no idea how she'd get his vehicle back to him. All she knew was she couldn't stay there a second longer after he dropped that bombshell on her.

Only it wasn't a bombshell. It was something she'd always known, and she was embarrassed and humiliated that she had wrongly assumed his feelings about marriage would change now they were in love.

It was insulting. Debasing. Killer painful.

She drove recklessly home through the dark streets, thankful that there was little traffic as tears blurred her vision.

At home, she stumbled into her bedroom and fell on the bed, sobbing with huge, aching sobs that racked her body until she fell asleep, emotionally exhausted.

25

Mitch watched Kerri peel out in his vehicle and shoved a hand into his hair, holding the back of his head. His gut cramped. Shit.

He rubbed his face as he stood leaning against the doorframe, watching the red taillights disappear. Maybe he could have handled that better. He knew that was a sensitive topic. But, he defended himself, she also knew he had no intention of ever getting married. Why on earth would she think he would change his mind?

He shut the door as he moved back into his dark, silent house, even emptier without Kerri there. Lately, if she wasn't at his place, he was at hers. He was getting used to her being around all the time.

He dropped down onto his couch, knees spread, hands hanging down between them, head bowed. The last thing he'd ever wanted to do was hurt Kerri. He almost groaned with the pain of having hurt her. He straightened and rubbed his chest, peered at the ceiling.

Maybe she'd get over it. He'd go over tomorrow to get his vehicle and talk to her. She'd be less emotional and they'd be able to talk about it rationally. There was no reason they couldn't go on just as they had been. Things were great. Maybe they could even move in together at some point. He might be okay with that, even though admittedly that wasn't a far cry from marriage.

But it was different. The expectations were less, there was no anticipation that living together would be forever, setting them up for a spectacular, hostile failure.

⚜

"They've all been using it!" Sela flattened her hands on Kerri's desk and leaned toward her, her face flushed and eyes flashing.

Kerri shrunk back in her chair and watched her sister numbly.

"All of them? All the massage therapists?" she clarified.

"Yes! And apparently it came from you! I cannot believe this. Why the hell would you do something like that behind my back?"

The secret massage oil was out. Kerri sighed, but after what had happened with Mitch on the weekend, it was hard to get too worked up about massage oil.

"It's really not that big a deal, Sela," she said dully. "Chill."

Sela's face reddened even more and she straightened, clenching her hands into fists at her side. "Chill! Kerri, you are way too laid back. I don't know how you run a business like that. You can't just do things like that…what if someone had some kind of horrible allergic reaction? We can't be using products without making sure they're safe and tested."

"Has anybody had a reaction?"

"Well, no. But they could have."

"The products are all natural botanical ingredients, pure and simple and safe. Not only that, I didn't actually intend for your massage therapists to use them on clients. I gave some oil to Amanda once to try on herself. I didn't know she was going to start using it here."

"But you kept giving it to her!"

Kerri's mouth turned down. "Yes, I did. Because her clients loved it and kept asking for it." She sighed. "I'm sorry, Sela. I know you like to control every detail of your business, but it just didn't seem that big of a deal. And it seemed to be a popular thing; I thought it was actually helping your business."

"My business doesn't need your help!"

"You know, I think you've been under a lot of stress lately. You are really overreacting to this."

Sela looked even more outraged, apparently annoyed by Kerri's calm reaction.

"While we're having this discussion," Sela continued tightly. "I've noticed all the stuff you put in the lounge. The Buddha statue has got to go. Same with the tinkling little water fountain. It's annoying. And your plants can go back into your studio or your office. If I want plants, I'll get my own plants."

Kerri just stared at her. "You've got to be kidding."

Sela shook her head. "You are leasing space here, and I'm the boss. If you want to make any changes that impact *my* business, you come see *me*. Got it?"

Despite her numb detachment from the situation, a little spiral of anger started deep down inside. Her sister thought she could walk all over her and call all the shots. Well, not any more. She was so tired of people thinking she was flaky, with no mind of her own and no need to be taken seriously. Despite Mitch's compliments the other day, he clearly felt that her desire to be married and have a family was inconsequential.

She stood up. "You are not my boss," she told Sela clearly and coldly. "Do not ever say that again, and do not even *think* that. I am my *own* boss. I apologized for doing things without your knowledge, but I was only trying to make things better. My clients come here, too. You are totally overreacting, which just shows what a stressed-out control freak you are."

"Control freak!" Sela sputtered. "Well, at least I have a profitable business. *You* wouldn't even have a business if it weren't for my help, after losing your lease."

That kind of stung, mostly because it was true. No. Kerri shook her head. It wasn't true. She would have found a way to keep going even if Sela hadn't come along with her offer to share space.

And what the hell did Sela know? Her yoga business was making money. Maybe not seven figures like the day spa, but it was making her very comfortable, thank you, even with having hired two instructors.

She narrowed her eyes at Sela angrily. "I don't need your help."

They glared at each other for a long moment, then Sela turned with a huff and exited Kerri's office. Kerri stared after her, throat aching, eyes burning.

Suddenly it all seemed too much. Mitch's hurtful refusal to commit to her despite the fact that he said he loved her, and her sister's cutting words were just too much to bear.

Tears stung her eyes as she leaned against the edge of her desk, staring blindly into space.

She hadn't wanted that much. A man to love, to spend her life with, make a family with. Respect from her family and friends. And sure, a successful business, although she already knew her definition of success was different than Sela's and maybe her parents', and maybe even Mitch's. Everyone was so focused on money and profits. Kerri liked the fact that she was making a difference in people's lives.

Even with the stupid massage oil. She'd been so proud of the formulas she'd developed and how popular they had been. Even the fact that Amanda had apparently given the oil to the other therapists and *they* too were using it was a compliment to her abilities. Nobody seemed to recognize that.

Nobody would ever take her seriously now.

Glumly, she contemplated her office, blinking back tears.

Clearly this wasn't going to work out with her and Sela in the same space. For some reason, Sela thought that gave her the right to criticize and tell her how to run her yoga busines. Kerri sighed. Back to the drawing board. She'd have to start again looking for some space for a studio.

It was going to be even harder now, though, because she'd added all those classes, which were really popular. People liked it here — the warm décor, comfortable waiting area and changing rooms, and all that parking. She sighed.

She shoved a hand wearily through her hair. She was emotionally drained from her disagreement with Mitch and now this. She'd lost her best friend, the love of her life that she'd only just found, and now her business was in jeopardy too. Shit.

She glanced at her watch. She had one more class today and then she could go home and hide and maybe she'd never come out.

She couldn't get out of it.

Kerri sighed. Hailey had convinced her to make an appearance at the birthday party she was throwing for Miguel, even though she knew Mitch was going to be there. Kerri hadn't wanted to talk about what had happened between her and Mitch, so she hadn't told Hailey about their break-up. It was too humiliating. She was completely, helplessly in love with a man who refused to marry her.

But when she'd refused to come to the party, she'd had to tell Hailey something. Too bad Hailey's sympathy just made her start crying all over again, when she'd thought she had finally cried herself dry and gotten control.

Now here she was walking into Hailey's home, knowing she was about to see Mitch, her stomach in tight knots, her mind a whirl of frantic thoughts.

Her eyes searched the room even as she greeted her friends and followed Hailey into the kitchen. She didn't see Mitch.

"He's not here yet," Hailey told her in a low voice. "I haven't said anything about you two breaking up, but everyone's going to wonder why you're here without him. Someone's going to ask where Mitch is."

"Oh, God." Kerri pressed a hand to her stomach. "What should I say?"

"Just keep it simple." Hailey handed her a glass of wine. "Just say you're not together any more and you think he's coming later."

Kerri nodded. She went back out to mingle with friends, her eyes constantly going to the door every time someone came in. She tried to laugh and talk and pretend her life wasn't crumbling, tried to keep the sadness from swamping her. Luckily, Jason and his wife had just announced they were pregnant, which focused everyone's attention on them.

She was talking to Jason's wife about the baby, and strangely, she wasn't even envious. Usually when someone was pregnant, she had to fight off feelings of jealousy because that was something she wanted so badly.

Was it possible that if she didn't have Mitch, it didn't matter if she had kids?

Whoa. That was a radical mind shift for her. But a baby didn't seem like such a big priority when she was so miserable from missing Mitch.

It wasn't the best time for Mitch to finally show up. He walked in looking all tall, big and gorgeous, smiling at Hailey, clapping Miguel on the back and wishing him happy birthday.

Kerri couldn't take her eyes off him. Her heart squeezed

painfully and she could hardly breathe. He hadn't noticed her yet, so she could watch him. He didn't look like the happiest guy in the world either. Well, good.

She turned back to Marla with a bright smile. "So, do you want a boy or a girl?"

Marla laughed. "I know I'm supposed to say I just want a healthy baby, but the truth is, I really want a little girl!" She chatted on while Kerri put on a show of listening and talking animatedly in case Mitch looked over.

When she glanced back to where he'd been standing, he was gone. She swallowed, and she and Marla and Hailey continued their baby discussion. She turned her empty glass in her hands and wished desperately for another drink, but she was afraid to get up and go get one in case she ran into Mitch.

"Hailey?" she murmured. "Would you be a super friend and get me another glass of wine?"

Hailey just looked at her. "Sure. You just hide here in your corner all night."

Sarcasm. Whatever. Kerri was totally fine with just hiding there in her corner all night.

Eventually Mitch reappeared in the room and, like magnets, their gazes collided instantly, sending a jolt through her like a live current. The music, the loud chatter of voices fell away, and all she could see was his face — sober, serious, mouth straight, eyes shadowed. Kerri's lips trembled and her throat hurt. Her chest ached painfully.

I can't do this. I cannot do this. No, I have to do this. She wanted to flee, but some small remnant of pride made her stay where she was, leaning down to hear Marla's latest comment. She laughed, tearing her eyes from Mitch's, and flipped her hair back from her face. Even as she did that, she recalled him teasing her about flipping her hair and slowly lowered her hand with a little heart stab.

She downed the rest of her wine and stood, happy now to have a reason to escape the room.

There was a second smaller party going on in the kitchen, as usual. Hailey was getting some food ready to serve. "Can I help?" Kerri asked desperately.

"Sure." Hailey handed her a bowl of chips. "Go take this to Mitch."

"Huh?" She stared at her friend, dumbfounded.

"I'm kidding." Then Hailey muttered, "Sort of."

Kerri took the bowl from her friend and said in a low voice, "Are you trying to tell me I should talk to him?"

Hailey looked back at her, her face sad. "You guys had something special. I just think you could still work things out if you just talked."

"I don't want to talk to him," she said through clenched teeth, and turned and stalked away. She strode into the living room, flung the bowl of chips down onto a table, and walked out again. Fighting back tears, she headed down the hall to the bathroom. Someone was in there, so she stumbled into Hailey's bedroom and sat down on the edge of the bed, trying not to sob. God, this was hard.

She was sitting in the dark when the open doorway filled with a large body silhouetted against the hall light. She recognized Mitch's form even though she couldn't see his face.

"Are you okay?" he asked in a low voice.

Desperately she blinked back tears and forced a smile. "Of course," she said brightly. "Just waiting to use the bathroom."

"Kerri..."

"Just go away, Mitch."

"But...we need to talk. I was going to talk to you on Sunday when I came to get my vehicle, but you'd already brought it back. I tried to call you..."

"There's nothing to talk about." She shrugged. "Don't worry about it."

"But..."

The bathroom door opened and Kerri jumped to her

feet. "Excuse me." She waited for Mitch to move and let her out of the bedroom. He didn't budge. She stood there. They stared at each other, tension crackling between them.

Her heart was breaking, literally shattering. A sob rose and she caught her breath, trying to hold it in, making a little hiccup noise. She swallowed hard. As someone passed them in the hallway, she shoved past Mitch and darted into the bathroom, closed and locked the door behind her.

Shit, shit, shit. Now she was trapped in there all night. She leaned on the marble vanity, taking deep breaths, fighting for control. If she could just get out of there without crying and humiliating herself, she could slip out the front door and leave the party.

She stared at herself in the mirror, her cheeks flushed pink with the effort not to cry, eyes glistening and full of pain. Her mouth was pinched tightly together. God, get a grip, she told herself.

She borrowed Hailey's hairbrush and dragged it through her hair, then ran her hands under cold water and pressed them to her hot cheeks. When she felt she looked relatively normal, she left the bathroom, praying Mitch hadn't waited in the hall. There was no sign of him, so she found her purse and quietly left the party without even saying good-bye to Hailey and Miguel. Right now it was all about survival with her dignity intact.

26

Mitch had no patience for this particular client today. The guy was such a pathetic case, in love with his wife to the point of being a pushover, willing to give her almost everything she asked for in the divorce, which was a lot, all in the hopes that she would come back to him. Mitch had talked to Kerri about this client and his frustrations with him.

Now, here he was sitting in Mitch's office *crying*, for Christ's sake. Okay, not sobbing-out-loud crying, but he was definitely choked up and glassy-eyed.

Mitch sighed.

He did not need all this emotional crap. Probably because his own emotions were all over the place and so close to the surface he was ready to snap. In fact, he'd barked at Christie earlier when she'd accidentally brought him the wrong file. Shit.

He scrubbed a hand over his face.

"Look, Gord," he said wearily. "You don't have to give in that quickly. We can do better than this. You need to think of the long-term ramifications."

"I just want her to be happy." Gord looked at Mitch. "I love her, Mitch. I wish I didn't, but I do. I'm miserable without her and the thought that I'm going to have to spend the rest of my life without her is killing me, man."

"Yeah," Mitch said morosely, without really thinking. "I know what you mean."

Gord glanced at him. "Are you divorced? I didn't know that."

Mitch shook his head. "No. I'm not divorced. I just know what you mean about having to spend the rest of your life without her."

"Oh. Then you don't really know what I mean."

"Uh...yeah. I do." Why the hell was he arguing? It pissed him off that this guy thought he had cornered the market on grief and misery just because he was getting a divorce. Was it any less painful to lose your best friend and the woman you loved so much it hurt, just because you weren't actually married?

Whoa. That was a crazy thought. He tried to follow that train despite his brain cramping up. If he and Kerri were married and splitting up, would it hurt any more than this? He couldn't see how. So, hey, they might as well be married.

Oh Christ.

He wanted to be with Kerri. All the time. The thought of her marrying another guy and having his children was like a dagger twisting in his gut. It had been driving him nuts ever since she'd begged him to help her find a husband, which had made him do all those crazy things. No way was some other guy having her. No fucking way.

He would marry her himself.

He gazed across his office, stunned and bewildered. He couldn't believe he'd just had that thought and no chills raced up and down his spine, no terror clutched at his chest, no nausea rolled in his stomach.

Mitch stood.

"I have to go," he said abruptly to his client.

Gord's forehead creased. "Huh? I just got here."

"Sorry. We'll reschedule. Something just came up."

CLOSEL

Kerri arrived at the studio early to go on the internet to look at commercial real estate listings again. Her kids' yoga class started in half an hour.

She scrolled down with a sigh. Everything was super expensive. She'd crunched the numbers and knew what she could afford but man, this was going to cut into her profits. She'd be eating macaroni and cheese for months.

Bah. She didn't need to eat. In the last two weeks, her appetite had disappeared to the point where her yoga pants hung so loosely on her hips she'd almost lost them in the men's class doing Downward-Facing Dog.

It was too much effort to care. So she'd flashed a little lace thong at them. It was probably good for business.

"Hey," came a voice from her door. She lifted her head to see Sela. They hadn't spoken much in the last few days, although Kerri had quietly removed her Buddha and water fountain and plants from the waiting room. She'd taken the remainder of the herbal teas she'd purchased as well, feeling petty because there were only like, three tea bags left and who cared, but hell, if Sela was pissed off about it, fine.

Amanda had been almost in tears at what had happened, apologizing to Kerri for the uproar. The secret had come out when a client came in wanting to purchase a bottle of the oil. Of course, the girls at the front desk had had no idea what she'd been talking about and called Sela, who also had no idea but quickly figured it out. The woman kept insisting she'd "seen it in a magazine".

Lines bracketed Sela's mouth and her eyes tightened. "Can I talk to you for a few minutes?"

Kerri checked her watch. "I have about half an hour before class."

Sela pulled up a chair and tossed a glossy women's magazine down on Kerri's desk. "I came to apologize," Sela said, with obvious difficulty. "I'm very sorry about the things I said to you the other day."

Now *this* was a surprise.

"Oookay," Kerri said slowly. "I guess I'm sorry, too, then, for calling you a control freak."

"No." Sela rubbed the back of her neck. "I *am* a control freak. I was out of line to criticize your business. You're right. I'm not your boss." She paused. "And I *am* stressed. Do you...do you think a yoga class would help me?"

Kerri stared at her in amazement. "Do you have time for that? You're always going nuts, between here and home."

"I'll find time. I *need* to find time. I need your help, Kerri. The harder I try to control things, the more out of control I feel."

Kerri nodded, eyeing her sister thoughtfully. "Sure, I'll help, Sela, if you really mean that. I just can't believe...you're the one who can do it all, even with one arm tied behind your back."

Sela let out a shaky breath. "Doug and the girls are angry because I'm never home lately, and I'm stressed to the max trying to get things going here. I thought I was doing a good job of managing everything, but I think I'm just doing a good job of killing myself."

"I offered to help," Kerri couldn't resist pointing out. "But you need to do it all."

"I need to learn to delegate better. We had a big blow out at home last night and I realized things have to change."

Wow, that was a huge thing for Sela to admit.

"And," she continued. "I owe you another apology." She pushed the magazine toward Kerri, folded open.

She pointed to a small article at the bottom of the page.

Kerri glanced at it, not really seeing it. She took another look. The article was a little promotional piece about the White Lotus Spa and Yoga Studio in Santa Barbara.

"Hey!" she said with delight. "That's us!"

"Mmhmm. Read it."

Kerri read it quickly. "This is nice!" Apparently a beauty editor at the magazine had visited the spa, unbeknownst to them. She'd had a few services and had loved them all, raved about the "incredibly silky, rejuvenating massage oil that made skin feel like polished silk, the fragrance mesmerizing and sexy". Kerri gave a little shiver of pleasure. The woman hadn't attended a yoga class, but had called and been told there were waiting lists for almost every class.

"I didn't know you had waiting lists. I just didn't realize how popular your classes are. And you've expanded so much, that makes it even more amazing."

"Why is it amazing?" She pushed the magazine back across the desk. "Why is everyone surprised that I can actually run a successful business?"

"That's not what I meant! I just meant, 'amazing' as in 'great'. Fantastic. Not that I'm surprised by what you've done."

Kerri grimaced, unsure if she believed her sister's protests.

"And the oil...obviously I made a big mistake there. You were totally right. People love it. They've been coming in and asking for it ever since this magazine came out last week."

"Great," Kerri said, both pleased and dismayed. "I can't exactly mass produce it in my kitchen."

Sela laughed. "Is that where you make it? I had no idea. So, I was thinking...maybe we *should* mass produce it. We could sell it here at the spa."

Kerri looked at her warily. She and Mitch had already

talked about that idea, but it had seemed a bit far-fetched. "Who's going to produce it? You? Or me?"

"Both of us. Partners."

Kerri shook her head. "I think we learned this week that we could never be partners. We're too different."

"Come on Kerri. I know I've been difficult, but a lot of it's the stress."

"No, a lot of is your anal, controlling personality."

Sela surprisingly didn't take offence. "I'm working on that. We could do it, Kerri. Come on."

"You want one of my business ideas," she said slowly.

"We'd have to work on a business case." Sela nodded. "Cost benefit analysis and all that. But I think it has huge potential."

"I do have other ideas for some skin care products...cleansers and moisturizers...shower gel, bath stuff..."

"That sounds great! We could have our own White Lotus line of beauty products."

"I don't know." Doubts still tapped at her with little hammers. "You're already on overload. How can you think about taking on more?"

"I was hoping you'd take on most of it." Sela eyed her hopefully. "I'll help with financing and anything else you need from me, but I'd like you to run with it. If you're interested."

Yeah, she was interested, but it was hard to believe Sela could contribute financially to a project and not want a say in every small decision.

Sela frowned, looking at Kerri's computer screen. "Are you...what are you looking for, Kerri?"

"New space." Kerri glanced at the monitor. "After last week I thought it might be best if I find somewhere else for my studio."

"Oh, no." Sela sat up straight and her brows drew

down. "I'm so sorry, Kerri. I didn't mean to drive you away. Really, I didn't. I just lost my cool."

Kerri nodded. Her sister did seem genuinely remorseful.

"Don't go," Sela begged. "You've been a huge benefit to my business."

"I have?"

"Yes! You're such a…special person, you draw people in. I've had so many people coming to the spa that are your clients, and with the popularity of that massage oil…it's been great. Plus, I have to tell you that when you took your stuff out of the lounge, a couple of clients commented that it felt different in there."

Kerri smiled slowly. She so much wanted to say "I told you so", but restrained herself. She'd never had much chance to use that line as kids because Sela was invariably right, but now she felt a flood of warm pride that Sela had recognized *she* had been right about something.

"I guess we can keep trying," she said slowly. "I just…I always feel so inferior to you, Sela. You have it all—a great husband, family, your business—and Mom and Dad just think you're the sun and the moon. Maybe it would be better if I were on my own again."

Sela tipped her head to one side. "Mom and Dad think *you're* the special one. They're always harping on me to not work so hard. They think I neglect my family and I'm too focused on money."

Now Kerri shook her head. "You have got to be kidding me."

Sela shook her head, too. "No, I'm not."

"They've never said anything like that to me."

Sela grinned. "That's the great thing about our parents. They might try to tell us what we're doing wrong, but at least they do it to our faces. They don't criticize us behind our backs. They're nothing but supportive of you and Justin and Jared when they talk to me."

"Yeah. That's true." Kerri took a deep breath and glanced at her watch. "Oh, God, I have to go. My kids are waiting." She looked at her sister. "Thanks, Sela."

Sela smiled. "I'm sorry again. Please, think about it. I don't want you to go."

The kids were running around the studio, balls of energy bouncing off the walls, rolling around on the floor mats and giggling and yelling. Kerri grinned. She couldn't help but feel energized by their joyful exuberance.

Kerri focused herself and soon the kids sat quietly, practicing their "balloon breath". She took them through the fun poses, the class louder and more active than her adult classes. They did the cobra snake, hissing enthusiastically, the elephant, making nasal roaring noises, and the fish, popping their lips in exaggerated fish kisses. Kerri laughed and made the noises along with them.

She was opening and closing her mouth in huge fishy kisses when she happened to look up to see Mitch standing at the door, watching through the window. He was leaning against the door frame, arms crossed across his broad chest, smiling faintly, and her heart gave a little bump at the sight of him. She closed her mouth abruptly, mildly embarrassed, then refocused herself on the class.

The children lay down for the shavasana, arms at their sides, eyes closed, and Kerri laid there quietly herself, keeping an eye out for anyone who might not be so relaxed. That would be her, actually. Knowing Mitch was watching her was testing her ability to focus inward and harmonize mind, body and spirit. Okay, it shot that ability all to hell.

27

itch grinned as he watched Kerri's lush little mouth popping like a fish. The kids were all doing it too, and it was hilarious. Kerri rose to correct one little girl's posture with a gentle hand on her back, then surveyed everyone else to ensure they were doing the pose correctly. She smiled at the kids with genuine affection, and something grabbed at his gut.

She would be a great mother. You could just tell she really loved kids and was so comfortable with them, down on the floor with them, joining them in their goofy antics and laughing.

When they were finished, he watched with charmed amusement as many of the kids ran up to Kerri for a hug before they left. Mitch became aware of all the mothers in the hall around him, waiting for their children to come bursting out.

"Isn't it amazing how the yoga calms them down?" one mother said to another.

"Oh, yeah." She nodded vigorously. "There is such a difference in Rachel's ability to focus lately. Kerri's so good with them."

He glanced at them, then back at Kerri with a warm feeling of pride. When the room emptied, he stepped in and closed the door behind him. Kerri was picking up mats and cushions.

"Hi."

She looked up at him solemnly. "Hi. What are you doing here?"

He didn't answer right away but started helping her put things away. "Can we talk?"

"About what?"

"About us."

"I don't know." She pushed her hair off her face. She looked tired and a bit drawn, but still stunningly beautiful. "I'm a bit overloaded at the moment."

"How come?"

Her gaze was steady but wary. "Stuff."

He rolled his lips in. "Please. I need to talk to you. You won't take my calls, and you've been avoiding me. We have to talk."

She gave a tiny nod and led the way through the side door of the studio into her office. She took the seat on the other side of the desk, out of touching range, damn it. His hands ached to feel her, his body needed her.

He sat down, feeling stiff as a plank compared to her easy grace.

"So talk," she invited in a cool and uninviting tone.

Now he was there and actually had her attention, the words evaporated. He swallowed. "Kerri, I was wrong—" he began.

"Holy shit!"

He started and lifted his gaze to her.

Her face wore a look of exaggerated astonishment. "Are you okay? I don't think I've ever heard those words come out of your mouth before."

He scowled. "You're not making this any easier."

"Why should I?" she muttered.

He dragged in a deep breath. "I love you, Kerri. I want to be with you, and most of all, I don't want anyone else to be with you. You think you need a husband? Fine, then—it's going to be me."

She stared at him, her mouth gaping open. She snapped it shut.

"Yesterday I had a meeting with a client. Remember the guy who still wanted to get back with his wife and was giving her everything under the sun?" She nodded, eyes shuttered. "Well, we were talking and I realized it doesn't matter if we're married or not—being without you hurts. I love you and I want to be with you for the rest of our lives and if I can't be with you... Hell, I don't know how to say this."

He watched her swallow and lick her lips in a sexy way. "Are you saying...you want to get married? Or are you still trying to convince me we can be together without being married?"

"I'm saying I want to marry you."

He could not believe what had just came out of his mouth. He had never in his life thought he would ever say those words. A painfully heavy silence hung between them for long heartbeats.

"Well," she said eventually. He'd expected a bit more of a thrilled reaction from her.

"Uh..."

She still just gazed at him. "The thing is," she finally said. "I don't think I need to get married any more."

"Huh?" He didn't get it. "What the hell does that mean, you don't *need* to get married?"

She gave a crooked little smile. "Turns out my family apparently does respect me."

What did that have to do with marriage? Sometimes she really was flaky. He gave his head a shake.

"I don't need a husband and a family to be taken seriously. I am a successful, independent woman."

"Yes, you are," he agreed, still bewildered. "But...is *that* why you wanted to get married?"

She nodded, looking a little abashed. "That's part of it. I do want to have a family and I'm not getting any younger, but I..." She focused on her hands. "I felt like nobody took me seriously. All the stuff I've done... I know my business isn't as big as Sela's, but I do okay. My parents treat her like an adult and they treat me like a little kid. I just thought if I was a married woman, a mother...they would know that I'm grown up. They would treat me like an adult, respect the things I've done."

Mitch studied her for a long moment, not sure what to say. Was *that* what this whole marriage thing had been about? He couldn't believe someone so together, someone as smart and funny and special as Kerri could have had doubts like that about herself.

"Kerri, you are most definitely all grown up." His throat felt like he had a popcorn kernel stuck there. He gave a little cough. "I'm just...mind-boggled you could think that. So, what happened to make you realize that's crazy?"

"Sela and I had a big fight the other day, about her trying to control my business and me interfering in hers."

"Ah. The massage oil issue. I gather she found out."

"Oh yeah. And was she ever pissed! Some beauty editor from Lux magazine came to the spa and had a massage with one of my oils. She raved about it and wrote a promo piece in the magazine about our spa. Then people started calling here and asking for the stuff. That's how Sela found out."

He nodded.

"But it's actually a good thing. When she found out about the article, she wasn't so mad, because it is good publicity after all. Free advertising. So, she apologized. She really overreacted because she's been so stressed about the move and everything. Sounds like her family is going to make her change some things. I *knew* she was overdoing it." She shook her head. "And she actually proposed that we start producing some of my oils and other skin care products — remember, you and I talked about that?"

"Yeah, I remember." He smiled, warm pride rushing through him.

"She also told me that Mom and Dad *do* think I'm doing a good job," she continued softly. "So getting married just to show them how together I am is probably not the best idea. I thought I needed to do that, but now I know that was just crazy. Besides, you don't really want to get married. You're just saying that."

"Kerri, why would I say that if I didn't mean it? God, *me* of all people."

She nodded. "You're just trying to make me happy."

"Is that...bad?"

She smiled slowly. "No. I love it. I love you. But I don't want to make you miserable. If you don't want to get married, I'm fine with that. We can be together and...just...be together."

"What about...kids? You know you want to be a mother. You *should* be a mother."

Her smile softened, touched with a hint of sadness. "Yeah. But if it never happens, I'd be okay with that. It would be...you know...karma. I think I can live without kids." She hesitated, took a breath. "But I don't think I can live without you."

He felt like a fist squeezed his throat. Ah, hell. That was how he felt, too. Now he *had* to touch her. He rose up out of the chair and strode behind her desk. He pulled her up out of her chair, and they stood there, his hands holding hers, tightly pressed between their bodies.

"I don't want you to give that up," he said. "You want kids and I want them to be mine. Nobody else's."

"Well, I wasn't going to go to a sperm donor or anything."

He snorted. "Jesus. That's not what I meant. I just...I told you before that it was driving me crazy thinking of you with other guys, maybe marrying some other guy. I can't let you do that. You're mine and I'm going to marry you and that's it."

"Oooh. I love it when you get all possessive and dominating." She gave him a wicked little smile. She pulled her hands from his and wound her arms around his neck. He set his hands on her waist, tugged her closer. She smelled so damn good, that ylang-ylang stuff making him want to eat her up. Her blue eyes sparkled, captivated him as always. "You know, most guys *ask* a girl to marry them."

"Forget it," he dismissed. "Not giving you a chance to say no. Besides, I know you want to marry me."

"Arrogant," she murmured, lips curving into an enticing smile.

"Let's go do it right now," he challenged her.

Her eyes widened, then she laughed. "Yeah, right."

"I'm serious." He reached into his back pocket and pulled out some papers, folded thickly into quarters. He handed them to her.

She took the papers, gazing at him with curiosity. She unfolded them and read, then read again. She looked up at him, eyes wide and crystalline blue. "What is this?" she asked, her voice husky. "Airline tickets?"

He nodded.

"To...Paris?"

"Yep. Leaving Monday."

"But...I can't...we can't...Mitch, you're crazy."

He grinned. "We're going on a honeymoon. I couldn't get the marriage license without you, but we can do that Monday morning."

"Oh. My. God." She stared at him, then threw herself against him, stood on her tiptoes to reach his mouth, giving him a long, deep, hungry kiss, fingers threading through his hair to pull his head closer. He held her close, kissed her back thankfully, with huge relief and all the love and lust and friendship he had for her.

She pulled back to look at him, mouth wet and swollen from their kisses. God she was sexy. And adorable. And smart.

"Why are lawyers' graves forty feet deep instead of the traditional six feet deep?" Kerri asked him, arms still around his neck.

Thrown off balance for a moment, he gave his head a little shake. "Oh, God. Why?"

"Because really deep down, lawyers are not such bad guys."

He groaned.

"Sorry," she said softly, her mouth touching his. "But I really mean that. I love you so much. Now we really are friends with benefits."

He drew back with a glower, and she smiled. "You're still my best friend." She laid one hand on his cheek. "But so much more than that. Now I have *all* the benefits—not just the sex. Benefits like love and friendship and commitment and…"

"And sex…"

She frowned, and he laughed and kissed the frown away. "I know, I know," he said. "*All* the benefits."

Bonus Content

Enjoy this interview with Kerri and Mitch
after they return from their honeymoon in Paris!

Kelly: So tell us all about your honeymoon in Paris!

Kerri: It was soooo romantic. *(Glances at Mitch)*. Until Mitch had an anxiety attack about getting married.

Mitch: I did not have an anxiety attack!

Kerri: What was it then? I swear you were having cold feet because we got married so fast.

Mitch: I ate some bad pâté. That stuff is disgusting.

Kerri: Can't say I was fond of it either, but otherwise the food was amazing.

Mitch: Kerri even ate bread.

Kerri: *(laughing)* Yes I did and you could not believe how much better bread tastes in France. Every day we'd stop in the middle of the afternoon at one of the little brasseries and sit outside and have a glass of wine and watch people. It was so beautiful.

Kelly: I went to Paris a few years ago and I loved it.

Kerri: I loved it too. It really was romantic. I love the history and the old buildings. I loved looking down these narrow old streets, lined with buildings and imagining who lives there. And how many people have lived there over the years.

Kelly: Did you do all the tourist things? Notre Dame? The Louvre? Versailles? The Eiffel Tower?

Kerri: Yes! We even went to the top of the Eiffel Tower.

Mitch: But you got scared and we had to go down.

Kerri: *(frowning)* Who knew I was afraid of heights? And all the security made me nervous.

Mitch: Then we looked at a lot of old paintings at the Louvre and Versailles.

Kerri: There's so much history. It's mind-boggling to think that people actually lived in a place like that. The Louvre was actually a palace, too, until um…

Mitch: 1672

Kerri: Yes, thank you. In 1672 Louis XIV moved to Versailles from the Louvre which then became a place to display the royal collection.

Kelly: What was the best part of your trip?

Mitch: The sex.

Kerri: Mitch!

Mitch: You deny it?

Kerri: Okay, no. But it was also very romantic sitting at a sidewalk brasserie having dinner one evening at dusk and watching the lights on the Eiffel tower come on. It's quite a show. Walking down the Champs-Élysées under the chestnut trees. And then on the way back to the hotel on the subway, some guy just started playing jazz music on a saxophone. He was so good!

Mitch: *(grinning)* Yeah, that was cool. But actually the best part was no lawyer jokes.

Kerri: Oh, that reminds me! How many lawyers does it take to change a light bulb?

Mitch: Oh my God.

Kelly: Um...how many?

Kerri: Fifty-four.

Mitch: Oh my God.

Kerri: Eight to argue, one to get a continuance, one to object, one to demur, two to research precedents, one to dictate a letter, one to stipulate, five to turn in their time cards, one to depose, one to write interrogatories, two to settle, one to order a secretary to change the bulb, and twenty-eight to bill for professional services.

Kelly: *(muffles laughter)*

Mitch: Okay. How about this: What did the Yogi say to the hot dog vendor?

Kerri: *(frowns)*

Mitch: Make me one with everything. (laughs)

Kerri: *(groaning)* Very funny.

Mitch: Hey, I think I owe you a few. In fact, I think I owe you a spanking for that last one.

Kerri: Oooh. Are we done here?

Author Note

Thank you so much for reading *Friends With Benefits*! Make sure you're on my mailing list for news about my next releases. If you enjoyed Friends With Benefits, please consider leaving a review at the retailer of your choice or at Goodreads to help other readers find my books. You can also contact me at info@kellyjamieson.com to tell me what you thought of it or ask me any questions!

Other Books by Kelly Jamieson

Heller Brothers Hockey
Breakaway
Faceoff
One Man Advantage
Hat Trick
Offside

Love Me
Friends with Benefits
Love Me More
2 Hot 2 Handle
Lost and Found
One Wicked Night
Sweet Deal
Hot Ride
Crazy Ever After
All I Want for Christmas
Sexpresso Night
Irish Sex Fairy
Conference Call
Rigger
You Really Got Me
How Sweet It Is

Power Series
Power Struggle
Taming Tara
Power Shift

About the Author

Kelly Jamieson is a best-selling author of over forty romance novels and novellas. Her writing has been described as "emotionally complex", "sweet and satisfying" and "blisteringly sexy". She likes coffee (black), wine (mostly white), shoes (high heels) and hockey!

Subscribe to her newsletter for updates about her new books and what's coming up, follow her on Twitter @KellyJamieson or on Facebook, visit her website at www.kellyjamieson.com or contact her by emailing info@kellyjamieson.com.